Invisible
and
Timesnatch

ROBERT SWINDELLS

Invisible
and
Timesnatch

CORGI YEARLING BOOKS

TIMESNATCH and INVISIBLE! 2-in-1
A CORGI YEARLING BOOK 0 440 86734 7

TIMESNATCH
First published in Great Britain in 1994 by Doubleday
an imprint of Random House Children's Books
Corgi Yearling edition published 1995, 2001

INVISIBLE!
First published in Great Britain in 1999 by Doubleday
an imprint of Random House Children's Books
Corgi Yearling edition published 2000

This 2-in-1 Corgi Yearling edition published 2005

1 3 5 7 9 10 8 6 4 2

Papers used by Random House Children's Books are natural, recyclable products
made from wood grown in sustainable forests. The manufacturing processes
conform to the environmental regulations of the country of origin.

Corgi Yearling Books are published by Random House Children's Books,
61–63 Uxbridge Road, London W5 5SA,
a division of The Random House Group Ltd,
in Australia by Random House Australia (Pty) Ltd,
20 Alfred Street, Milsons Point, Sydney, NSW 2061, Australia,
in New Zealand by Random House New Zealand Ltd,
18 Poland Road, Glenfield, Auckland 10, New Zealand,
and in South Africa by Random House (Pty) Ltd,
Isle of Houghton, Corner Boundary Road & Carse O'Gowrie,
Houghton 2198, South Africa

THE RANDOM HOUSE GROUP Limited Reg. No. 954009
www.kidsatrandomhouse.co.uk

A CIP catalogue record for this book is available from the British Library.

Printed and bound in Great Britain by
Bookmarque Ltd, Croydon, Surrey

Timesnatch

For Gabrielle

ONE

Butterflies don't know much. This one didn't know it was a chequered skipper – one of only sixty left in the world. It didn't know that this sun-dappled clearing was part of Rockingham Forest, and it certainly didn't know that its quick, darting flight was closely observed by three humans, two of whom weren't even born yet.

Heavy with the eggs it bore, the insect alighted on a leaf. At once the surrounding air became suffused with a soft, pulsating glow. The leaf trembled for an instant ever so faintly and when it stopped, the butterfly had gone.

'There you go, folks.' Harper Rye held up the flask for her children to see. 'One chequered skipper, extinct for twenty years yet very much alive, undamaged and beautifully pregnant. We've finally cracked it, my darlings.'

'Oh, Mum!' Kizzy, a ten-year-old version of her mother with the same straight dark hair and glasses, flung her arms round Harper's neck and kissed her on the mouth. 'I knew you'd do it. I *always* knew.'

'Steady!' Harper set down the flask before returning the child's embrace. 'Of course you did, my precious. Your faith in your old mum has been positively unswerving.'

'I knew you'd do it too,' growled Frazer. At thirteen he was less demonstrative than his sister and more cynical. 'What I *didn't* know was that you'd get all excited over butterflies and stuff when you could be snatching people. I mean, why can't we bring *Granny* back or something?'

Harper's grin faded as she looked at her son. 'Because, my love, the ability to create new technology carries with it heavy responsibilities. If we were to misuse my invention it might cause untold harm. For example, to snatch a human being – any human being – could alter history in some dramatic way we haven't even dreamed of. No.' She shook her head. 'Rule one *must* be – no humans.'

Frazer raked a hand through his mop of ginger curls. 'Hmmm. Never thought of that, Mum. Altering history, I mean. So that's why we're sticking to animals and plants – because that won't change history?'

'It *will*,' smiled Harper, 'but hopefully not in ways which will be harmful, or even particularly noticeable.'

Kizzy gazed at her mother's machine – a machine which could vanish and reappear like something in a magic show. It reminded her of an enormous doughnut. In fact, she'd christened it 'the Doughnut' without telling the other two. 'It's absolutely fantastic, Mum,' she breathed. 'What will you call it?'

'Oh – Rye's Apparatus, I expect. It's got a sort of ring to it, don't you think?'

Kizzy nodded. Better than the Doughnut, she thought.

'Rye's Apparatus.' Frazer rolled the words across his tongue a couple of times, then nodded. 'Ye-es. That sounds suitably historic, Ma – like Parkinson's Disease and Sod's Law. I reckon it'll do.'

Harper Rye laughed. 'I don't know about historic, my love. It might be best to keep this whole thing to ourselves, at least for the time being, but I know one thing – we'd better get this poor insect to Northamptonshire or it'll be forced to deposit its precious eggs in entirely the wrong place.'

TWO

It had begun four years earlier when physicist Harper Rye had noticed that certain subatomic particles were apparently capable of travelling back through time. At six, Kizzy had found the word 'physicist' too much to handle. As far as she was concerned, Mummy was a fizzy sister – a category which seemed to the child to describe her mother perfectly.

The initial discovery had given birth to an idea which had gripped Harper Rye, becoming almost an obsession. This in turn had triggered a successful application for funding to her old university, and a four-year bout of nonstop work which had driven her husband out of the family home in this isolated part of Suffolk and left the children very much to their own devices. For a couple of years they'd had a sort of nanny – a slow, amiable teenager named Pam who'd come from the village each morning to wash, dress and feed them, escort them to and from school and play with them, till she'd fallen in love and gone off to start a family of her own. They'd missed Pam terribly at first, but they'd learned to cope between them when Mum was busy, so that by the time Kizzy could say 'physicist' they were virtually independent.

Harper Rye's discovery had enabled her, after a tremendous amount of work, to design and construct a device which would travel back through time, snatch objects and convey them to her laboratory. The objects she intended to choose were plants and animals which once, not long ago, had inhabited the Earth but which had either been hunted or fished to extinction or wiped out by twentieth-century pesticides, urbanization or pollution. Her idea was to bring male and female specimens of such creatures into the cleaner, greener present, breed from them and release the offspring into the wild. In this way the consequences of past mistakes – of man's ecological vandalism – might be redeemed. Plants and animals which had vanished forever would reappear in 2039, enriching the earth once more with their variety.

And she'd done it, but not at first. At first, she'd encountered tremendous problems. There'd been problems of accuracy — of aiming her device at exactly the right spot at precisely the correct moment to capture a specimen. Then there'd been the problem of damage — precious specimens had arrived mangled or dead, or else in such a state of shock that they'd expired within a short time.

One by one the problems had been overcome, till now Harper Rye could guarantee to capture unharmed a creature as tiny, as fast-moving and as fragile as the chequered skipper which now rested inside its flask, the only chequered skipper in the world, as she drove the family car westwards along the A428 into Northamptonshire.

THREE

'Why d'you say we shouldn't tell anybody about your apparatus, Mum?' They'd released the butterfly and were cruising eastwards with the setting sun in the rearview mirror. The woman reached up and adjusted the glass till she lost the glare and found Frazer's puzzled face.

'You've read some history,' she said. 'Consider the fate of inventions. The aeroplane, for example. The first plane flew in nineteen hundred and three. The two guys who designed it probably thought they were giving the world a new, exciting sport or a fast, convenient means of getting from A to B. What they *didn't* foresee was that people would load bombs and guns on their machine and use it to slaughter one another, but that's exactly what they did.'

'Oh, yeah,' protested Frazer. 'But that was dead obvious, wasn't it? I mean, they should've known that would happen. I don't see how anybody could use Rye's Apparatus in a bad way.'

His mother smiled. '*You* don't see, darling, but believe me there are those out there who might.' She laughed briefly. 'You put an invention on the market – practically any invention – and somebody will find a way to use it as a weapon or to throw people out of work or to pollute the environment. When it comes to cruelty, greed and sheer stupidity, human ingenuity knows no bounds.'

Frazer pulled a face. 'Charming.'

'What'll happen to the butterfly?' asked Kizzy. The conversation was boring her. Her mother smiled. 'Well, my love, if we're lucky – *if* we're lucky – the butterfly will lay her eggs on a leaf. Hundreds of eggs. The eggs will hatch into hundreds of caterpillars, and some of those caterpillars – nine or ten perhaps – will survive to become butterflies next year. Those butterflies will mate and lay eggs and, before you know it, there'll be hundreds of chequered skippers in Rockingham Forest, just as there were a hundred years ago. But if we're *un*lucky,' she chuckled, 'a sparrow will eat our butterfly for breakfast first thing tomorrow morning.'

'Aw, Mu–um!'

'Well, darling, these things happen. We shan't know for ages, of course – a couple of years at least. Then, if no chequered skippers have been reported in the forest, we shall have to do the whole thing again.'

Frazer frowned. 'There's something I don't get.'

'*What* don't you get, dear?'

'The chequered skipper's extinct, right?'

'It *was*, yes.'

'Well – if it suddenly turns up again, won't people be curious? I mean, once a creature's extinct it's gone forever, isn't it?'

'Absolutely. But you see, darling, with something as tiny as the chequered skipper it's terribly hard to be certain. Nobody's *seen* one for twenty years, but when the species reappears they'll assume a few must've survived in a remote spot somewhere – that it wasn't extinct after all. That's why I chose to begin with something tiny.'

'Right.' Frazer grinned. 'It wouldn't work with a rhinoceros, would it?'

Harper shook her head. 'Not in Northamptonshire.'

They cruised on into dusk, laughing.

16

FOUR

The Ryes kept their secret for five months, during which time they re-established four species – two plants, a spider and an amphibian. It was while they were setting free their first birds that the trouble began.

It was a grey, blustery day in November. The Ryes had set off before dawn and had driven into Wales. At a remote location in the Brecon Beacons, Harper pulled over and switched off. It was almost midday but the road was deserted, the mountain landscape seemingly empty. The trio piled out of the Suzuki. Kizzy and

Frazer watched the road while their mother lifted out the basket. In the basket was a pair of red kites. Harper was unbuckling one of the straps which secured the lid when Kizzy hissed, 'Mum – look!' Harper glanced up. Two soldiers were approaching. 'Good Lord,' she murmured. 'Where on earth did *they* spring from?'

Kizzy shrugged. 'Out of the ground, it looked like.'

Her mother sighed. 'Never mind. Let me do the talking.'

'Morning.' The soldiers stepped on to the road. They weren't armed, but they didn't look particularly friendly. 'May I ask what you're doing?' one of them said.

Harper straightened up.

'Picnicking. Why – are we in a restricted zone or something?'

Instead of answering, the soldier nodded towards the basket. 'What's in there?'

'Food,' lied the physicist. 'Sandwiches and so forth. Why are you questioning us?'

'That's a livestock basket,' said the soldier. 'Odd thing to carry a picnic in. Open it, please.'

'Not till you tell me what this is about.'

'Madam, I must insist on your opening that basket.'

'And if I refuse?'

18

The soldier smiled fleetingly. 'Then *we'll* open it.'

Harper gazed at the man, who wore a captain's pips. 'What would you say, Captain, if I were to tell you that you were about to uncover a secret – a potentially dangerous secret?'

The captain smiled coldly. 'I'd say there is no such thing as a secret sandwich, nor a potentially dangerous sausage roll. Open the basket, please.'

'Oh, very well.' Harper squatted, undid the straps and raised the lid. A large bird rose in a clapping of wings to perch on the basket's rim. A loose feather whirled away on the wind. The captain gazed at the bird, then at the woman. 'Where did you get these creatures?'

Harper shook her head. 'I'm sorry, Captain – I can't tell you that.'

'Do you know what they *are*?'

'Yes. They're red kites.' As she spoke, the bird on the basket spread its wings, launched itself screeching into the air and wheeled away, followed at once by its mate. The second soldier side-stepped in a reflexive way with his arms spread, then, realizing the futility of his gesture, dropped his arms and stood watching the birds skim away, dwindling into the distance across a hillside. The captain said, 'The red kite was thought to be extinct. I must ask you once again how you came by these birds.'

'What *I* don't understand,' countered Harper, 'is what all this has to do with the Army. I mean – where did you spring from, and why are you so interested in birds, for goodness sake?'

'Most of this,' the captain indicated their surroundings with a sweep of his arm, 'is Ministry of Defence land. A lot of it is fenced off so people can't wander about, and it's become a sort of wildlife sanctuary.'

Harper chuckled. 'You're kidding, right?'

'No, I'm not.' The captain seemed nettled. 'Many rare species thrive on M.o.D. land. Some of them are found nowhere else, in fact, and we do what we can to protect them. That's why your basket worried us – it might have contained ferrets or falcons or something. We have to be careful, you see.'

'Good Lord.' The physicist shook her head. 'I must admit I've never thought of the Army as a guardian of the natural environment.' She looked at the captain. 'I think you'd better take me to your leader,' she said.

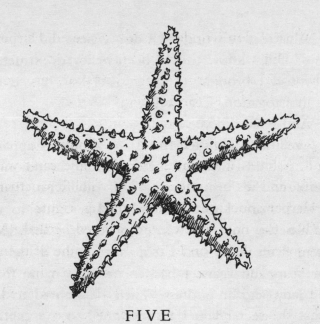

FIVE

'Where've you *been*, Mum?' demanded Kizzy as her mother climbed into the Suzuki. Frazer watched the army jeep do a three-point turn and speed away.

'I'm sorry, darlings.' The physicist fished for her keys. 'I'd no idea they'd keep me so long.'

'An hour and a half,' complained Kizzy. 'We thought you were never coming back.'

'What happened?' asked Frazer, as the jeep passed from sight.

'Oh.' His mother shrugged. 'They took me to see a colonel who asked me a lot of questions. Who was

I? What sort of work did I do? Where did I find the kites? Did I know they'd been believed extinct, and why had I brought them into Wales? It was quite an interrogation, I can tell you.'

'And what did you say?'

'Well, I couldn't tell the Army about my apparatus, so I'm afraid I invented a story. I told the colonel I'd inherited the birds from an old lady who died. It's a weak story, I know, but I had no time to think up a better one. He wanted to know where *she* got them from and I said I'd no idea – she'd had them for years and years. I had to invent a name for the old lady, and an address. Then he wanted to know what the secret was I'd mentioned to the captain. I said there *was* no secret – I'd just been hoping to make the captain leave us alone. Then he asked what I'd intended doing with the birds and I told him we meant to release them. I said the old lady had put it in her will that she wanted them released. He wrote everything down, but I don't think he believed me.'

'So what happens now?'

'I don't know, dear. I assume they'll check up, and when they find my old lady never existed they'll want to see me again.'

Frazer frowned. 'Doesn't that worry you, Mum?'

'Of course it does. The last thing I want is for the M.o.D. to come sniffing around, but if they do it can't be helped. All we can do is carry on with the work, keep our eyes open for strangers and hope to be left alone.' She turned the key in the ignition and steered the Suzuki on to the narrow mountain road.

Kizzy looked back. 'I wonder what those kites are doing now,' she said.

SIX

A few days before the Christmas holidays Frazer said, 'Mum, can I have Bilbo to stay for a night or two during the hols?' They'd heard nothing more from the Army and were beginning to relax. Bilbo, whose real name was Andrew Baggins, had once been Frazer's best friend.

Harper sighed. 'I suppose you may,' she said, 'since you stayed with him last summer, but I thought the two of you had fallen out?'

Frazer nodded glumly. 'We have, but you know

24

what he's like. He's absolutely nuts on pond-life and creepy-crawlies in general, and because that's *your* field he's been badgering the life out of me to invite him to spend some time here.'

His mother nodded. 'And of course he can use your stay with him as a lever.' She sighed again. 'I'll spend the whole time fending off his questions about my work, and you'll wear yourself out keeping him away from the lab and from certain outbuildings.'

'It'll be all right, Mum, honestly. Bilbo's interested in the Roman foundations they uncovered near Earl Soham, so we'll be out with our bikes a lot of the time, and at night you can tell him all about your creepy-crawlies without mentioning Rye's Apparatus.'

And so it was arranged. Andrew would arrive on the twenty-eighth of December and stay till the fourth of January. Kizzy was not pleased.

'Ooh, yuk!' she cried. 'I can't stand Andrew Baggins. He's creepy.'

Creepy or not, Andrew arrived at the Ryes' sprawling farmhouse on the twenty-eighth in his father's Volvo. Frazer and his mother helped take in their guest's baggage while Kizzy sulked in her room. Baggins senior drank a cup of coffee, said goodbye to his son and set off back to Bury St Edmunds.

'So, Mrs Rye,' said Bilbo as they turned from waving his father off. 'What are you working on these days?'

Groaning inwardly, Harper forced a smile. 'Oh, nothing dramatic, I'm afraid. Still chasing those elusive particles of mine.'

'Really?' Bilbo beamed. 'I look forward to hearing all about it, Mrs Rye. I'm totally *nuts* on particles, you know.'

Bilbo had arrived in mid-afternoon, and by the time he'd unpacked and settled into his room it was dusk. Over dinner they talked about particles. Frazer kept yawning and Kizzy was so bored she wished she dare flick some of her peas at their guest with her knife crying, 'How d'you like *these* particles, creep?' But of course, she daren't. After dinner the two boys went off to Frazer's room to play video games while Harper and Kizzy cleared up.

' 'Tisn't fair,' grumbled Kizzy. 'I never have a friend to stay. All *I* get to do is clean up after *his* friends.'

'Now, Kizzy,' smiled Harper. 'It isn't like that and you know it. Tomorrow it'll be their turn to do the washing-up, and you can have a friend to stay at Easter. How's that?'

Kizzy shrugged. 'I'll still be glad when he's gone.'

Harper bent, tea-towel in hand, to whisper in her daughter's ear. 'So shall I,' she said.

SEVEN

Things went well for three days. The weather was dry and mild and the two boys spent most of the daylight hours biking. They visited Earl Soham to view the excavations and did the round of nearby villages. In other circumstances Kizzy would have accompanied her brother, but she had no wish to go biking with Andrew Baggins. After dusk, Bilbo showed no inclination to investigate the house or its grounds, being perfectly content with Frazer's games and CDs.

At teatime on the thirty-first, Harper Rye said, 'As it's New Year's Eve I thought we'd push the boat out

– have a bit of a party.' While the boys had been out, she and Kizzy had prepared a feast, Kizzy having been bribed into helping by the promise of a slap-up feed for herself and a friend at Easter.

The festivities went well and the quartet greeted the new year in style. It was twenty to one when Harper mentioned the time and the party finally broke up.

Next morning, everybody slept late except Bilbo, who woke at his usual time of six-thirty. He lay for a while listening for sounds of his hosts rising, but heard nothing. At seven he got up and went downstairs. There was nobody about.

Bilbo was now where he hated to be – at a loose end. There was some washing-up to be done from last night and he did this, certain that the noise he made would rouse the household, but when the last teaspoon stood gleaming in the drainer, all was silent. 'Well,' he told himself, 'I'm not wiping 'em as well. I'm off exploring.'

He let himself out through the kitchen door and found himself standing in a cobbled yard enclosed on three sides by outbuildings. It was still dark, but the light from the kitchen window was enough to see by and he began strolling around, hands in pockets, trying doors and peering through dusty windows. Most of the doors yielded readily enough, revealing the sorts of things he'd expected: stepladders, coiled hoses, garden tools, broken toys, discarded furniture. One or two were locked, and looking through the windows of these revealed nothing because of the dark inside. It was when he reached the last building – a low, lime-washed structure not far from the door he'd come out by – that he found something which made him catch his breath.

The building had only one small window. Peering through this, the boy saw a long fishtank standing on a bench. The tank had a hood from which light fell, illuminating the interior. By this light, Bilbo saw that the water in the tank was only a few centimetres deep above a layer of gravel. Here and there, large pebbles broke the surface, and on these pebbles lay a number of creatures which he recognized as newts. This would have been only moderately interesting, except that Bilbo was almost certain he was looking at specimens of the great crested newt, an amphibian which had died out forty years before.

EIGHT

'Frazer?'

'Uh-huh?' It was nine-thirty. The two friends were biking north towards Thetford.

'You know that white building in your yard?'

'Sure. What about it?' Frazer's response sounded cool but his heart kicked.

'I looked through the window. There's a fishtank.'

'That's right.'

'With newts in it.'

'So?'

'I – they looked like great cresteds to me.'

'Don't talk daft, Bilbo. The great crested's extinct. What you saw were smooths. They have crests, y'know, and orange bellies, just like cresteds had.'

Bilbo shook his head. 'They were big, Frazer – far too long for smooths. I reckon they're great cresteds.'

Frazer scoffed. 'They *can't* be, can they? The crested's extinct, old mate. It's gone. Maybe the glass magnified 'em, or you saw two lying together. After all, it must've been pretty dark at the time.'

'What d'you keep 'em for, Frazer?'

'Pets. They're Kizzy's.'

'Why's the door locked, then?'

'I dunno, do I? Ask Kizzy.'

'I want to see 'em, Frazer. Close up, when we get back.'

Frazer shrugged. 'That'll be up to Kizzy, Bilbo. You'll have gathered she's not exactly crazy about you.'

Bilbo nodded. 'I've gathered, but I'll ask her anyway. After all, it's not a lot to ask, is it?'

'Kizzy?' It was three-thirty, and dusk. In the porch the boys had shed their mud-spattered footwear and were wiping down their machines.

Kizzy scowled at Bilbo. 'What?'

'I saw your newts this morning.'

'My—' She intercepted her brother's warning

32

glance and forced a smile. 'Oh, yes. My newts. Cute little beauties, aren't they?'

'I'd like to take a look at them if you don't mind.'

'But you've seen them, Andrew. You said so.'

'Close up, Kizzy. I want to see them close up.'

'Oh, but I've – I've put them to bed. In the wild, they'd be hibernating at this time of year. I have to be very careful, especially at night. Keep them warm. I'll show you in the morning if you like.'

Bilbo propped his gleaming bike against the lime-washed wall and shook his head. '*Now*, Kizzy. Show me now – I've never seen a great crested before.'

Kizzy laughed. 'Great crested? You won't see one of *those* in my collection, you div. They're extinct.'

'Then show me, Kizzy. Fetch the key and show me. It's just across the yard.'

'Hello, boys!' Harper appeared in the doorway, smiling brightly. 'Good ride?' She looked at Bilbo. 'Show you what, Andrew?'

'Oh – newts, Mrs Rye. I'd like to see Kizzy's newts.'

'Oh, yes. The newts. Fascinating creatures. First thing tomorrow, Andrew, OK? Dinner's ready now.'

NINE

Bilbo's room looked out on the yard. He spent some time gazing across at the white building before getting into bed. Then he lay for a while wondering whether it was worth sneaking down in an hour or so and trying to find a key. He decided it wasn't. There was probably only one key, and Kizzy would have it in her room. Drowsing, he began a fantasy in which he crept into Kizzy's room and retrieved it, but he fell asleep before the bit where he'd open the outhouse door.

Harper Rye was not asleep. She spent some minutes

with Kizzy, then went to her room and read till all was quiet. Then she crept downstairs, slipped into a parka and left the house through the kitchen door.

At breakfast Bilbo gave Kizzy a sly look and said, 'This is it then, Kizzy – the day we see the newts.'

Kizzy caught her lower lip in her teeth and gazed at her plate. When she didn't reply the boy said, 'Well, Kizzy – are you ready?'

'There are no newts, Andrew,' she murmured. 'I let them go.'

Bilbo stared. 'You let them go? On the second of January?'

Kizzy nodded.

'But they'll die. You said yourself they'd normally be in hibernation. Why on earth did you do it, Kizzy?'

The girl shook her head. 'I dunno. They were mine. I guess I just didn't want anyone to see them.'

'Meaning me?'

'Meaning anyone, Andrew.'

'Where are they – when did you do this?' Bilbo had risen to his feet as if he meant to rush off and rescue the amphibians.

'Andrew.' Harper Rye spoke softly. 'Sit down, please.' Bilbo sat and the woman said, 'What Kizzy has told you is not quite true, and that's my fault.'

35

'Y-your fault, Mrs Rye?'

'Yes. *I* removed the newts. I asked Kizzy to tell you she released them. I realize now that I was wrong. You deserve the truth, which is that the creatures form part of an experiment I'm conducting. The work is at a very sensitive stage, and I'd very much prefer not to exhibit the newts for the time being. I can tell you they are safe and well, and I'm sure I can rely on you to pursue the matter no further.'

Bilbo's nod was dubious. 'I – I won't talk about it, Mrs Rye, honestly, but I have to ask. *Are* they great cresteds?'

The woman nodded. 'Yes, Andrew, they are, but you mustn't ask where I found them.'

Bilbo stared at his hands on the tablecloth for a while, then swallowed hard and looked up. 'The great crested is extinct,' he croaked. 'There's only one place you *could* have found them.'

TEN

'So where is it?' persisted Bilbo, as he and Frazer pedalled without haste beneath an over-arching vault of naked branches.

'Where's what?' There was irritation in Frazer's tone. He was all right, old Bilbo, but he never knew when to back off.

'Your mum's device, whatever it is. The thing she used to bring those newts back to life.'

'Back to life?' scoffed Frazer. 'Who d'you think Mum is – Frankenstein?'

Bilbo shook his head. 'Quit stalling, OK? There are

extinct creatures at your place. Your mum admitted it and I saw 'em with my own eyes. Something's going on – something big, and I think scientists should come clean about what they're doing. It's secret work that produces sinister developments.'

Frazer sighed. Bilbo was due to go home the day after tomorrow. He wished it could be today.

'Listen, Bilbo. There's no device for bringing things back to life, right? You have my word on that. Mum found some great cresteds somewhere and she's working with them, and that's all I can tell you.'

'Well, it's not enough, old pal.' Bilbo's tone was angry. 'It's like there's a conspiracy between the three of you to hide the truth. Next time there's a phone box I'm going to call Dad and have him come for me. I won't stay where I'm not wanted.'

'Hey, Bilbo – there's no need—'

Bilbo began to pedal furiously so that Frazer found himself shouting at his friend's receding back.

'There's no conspiracy, you div. Mum's work's a bit hush-hush, that's all. She's a scientist, for Pete's sake.'

It was no use. Bilbo found a phone box at Woolpit and, by the time Frazer caught up, he'd done it. Remounting he said, 'I'm off back, Frazer. Packing to do. Dad's coming at six.'

It was a miserable ride. Bilbo set a cracking pace

and it took Frazer all his time to keep up. They didn't speak. When they got home, Bilbo marched through the house without a word to anyone and went straight to his room.

'What's up with *him*?' asked Kizzy. She and Harper were playing Scrabble.

Frazer told them what had happened.

'Oh, dear.' Harper levered herself out of the arm-chair. 'How embarrassing. Perhaps if I go up—'

'No, Mum.' Frazer shook his head. 'Leave him. It's no use. I know him. Once he's got something fixed in his skull, nothing'll budge it. I just hope his dad doesn't think we've been trying to poison him or something.'

'Oh, Frazer.' His mother hugged him. 'I'm so sorry. I hate to see my work coming between you and your friends like this.'

''S OK.' Frazer broke away. 'My own fault anyway – I invited him.'

Kizzy gazed across at them. 'I suppose this is what it'll be like from now on,' she said. 'Everyone avoiding us, saying, "Odd lot, those Ryes. Secretive. Something fishy going on there if you ask me."' She giggled. 'Could be quite fun in a way.'

ELEVEN

January gave way to February and February slipped into March, and the Ryes heard nothing from the Army. They began to relax. Each weekday Harper drove her children to school in Bury St Edmunds and collected them at the end of the day, and the hours between were filled with work.

One evening in mid-March, when the washing-up was done and the family was sitting round the log-fire, Harper said, 'Newts and butterflies are easy, but what about whales?'

'What about 'em?' asked Frazer.

'What about Easter?' queried Kizzy. 'Can I have Jennifer to stay like you promised?'

Harper sighed. 'Yes, darling, you can have Jennifer to stay exactly as I promised.' She smiled. 'There's plenty of room for Jennifer, but a pair of sperm whales is another matter entirely.'

'I wasn't going to invite any sperm whales,' giggled Kizzy. 'Just Jennifer.'

'Shut up, Kizzy,' growled Frazer. 'What's this about whales, Mum?'

'Well.' Harper bent forward and thrust a log of applewood into the embers. 'Up to now, the creatures we've snatched from the past have all been small, which is just as well. I mean, it's easy enough to keep an orchid here, or a tankful of newts or a pair of kites, but what about larger creatures? What about whales?'

Frazer shrugged. 'Can't do anything about 'em, can we? There's no sea here, and we can hardly shove two sperm whales in the back of the Suzuki and drive 'em down to Felixstowe.'

Kizzy looked thoughtful. 'No, but do they need to come here in the first place?'

Harper smiled. 'Go on, darling.'

'Well, what if you could snatch 'em from the past and have the Dough— I mean, have Rye's Apparatus deliver 'em straight to the seaside?'

'Why not indeed,' nodded Harper.

41

'Because it's not possible,' said Frazer. 'The specimens end up where the apparatus reappears, surely?'

His mother shook her head. 'Not necessarily, darling. Not any more. I've been slaving away all winter, using starfish.' She smiled. 'Yesterday I snatched a starfish from twenty-five years ago and placed it in the sea off Dunwich and it didn't even notice it'd moved.'

The boy gaped. 'So now you're thinking of—'

'Exactly. I'm thinking of locating some sperm whales, snatching a pair and slipping them into the ocean somewhere. I *think* our oceans have cleansed themselves of the muck our ancestors poured into them. Plankton populations are certainly up. I need to see whether whales can live in them once more.'

'But they'd be noticed, surely — things that size?'

Harper nodded. 'They'd be spotted eventually, no doubt. But so what?'

'So what?' Frazer looked at his mother. 'I thought this work of yours was supposed to be a deadly secret. Bilbo and I haven't spoken to each other for three months because of it, and now you're going to start scattering whales all over the place. You might as well put an ad in the paper and charge folk four ecu to see Rye's Apparatus in action.'

'Now, darling, don't exaggerate,' chided Harper. 'The ocean's a big place. When the whales are spotted, people will assume they've been hiding, that's all.'

'Are you sure, Mum? Won't it seem a bit strange, all these extinct species suddenly reappearing in pairs as though Noah's opened up his flipping Ark somewhere and let all the animals out?'

Harper laughed out loud and clapped her hands. 'What a wonderful image, darling. Noah's Ark. It'd never struck me, but that's exactly what Rye's Apparatus *is*, isn't it – a hi-tech Noah's Ark?' She shook her head. 'No, there's no danger. Even if someone *does* notice, a time machine's the *last* explanation they'll think of.' She grinned. 'I've decided there's such a thing as being *too* cautious.'

Frazer shrugged. 'Maybe you're right, Mum. I certainly hope so.' He chuckled. 'It only needs one Bilbo-type character to start putting two and two together and our secret's blown wide open.'

TWELVE

On April 3rd 2040, the following brief item appeared in the *Bury St Edmunds Gazette*:

> *Great crested newts, believed by scientists to have died out many years ago, have been found living in a pond near the village of Lenton. The discovery, made by children, is causing ripples in the scientific community, and the pond, known locally as Froglet Pond, has been designated a site of special scientific interest.*

THIRTEEN

On the first day of the Easter holidays, while Kizzy
entertained Jennifer and Frazer kept out of the way,
Andrew Baggins went to his local library. He pressed
the buzzer on the information desk and, when the assistant appeared, he handed her a newspaper clipping.

'This was in Wednesday's *Gazette*,' he said. 'Can
you tell me how to find out whether anything else
like that has been printed in other papers?'

The assistant read the item. 'You mean, about great
crested newts?'

Bilbo shook his head. 'No – about anything. Any

45

creature that was supposed to be extinct being seen alive.'

'Well—' The woman frowned. 'There's a computer service that searches for items under various headings, but whether it'll have anything about extinct creatures, I don't know. I could try it for you, but there's a charge and it might take a while.'

Bilbo nodded. 'That's OK. Shall I come back tomorrow?'

The assistant smiled. 'Better make it the day after. If there *is* anything, I'll have printouts ready for you then.'

'Fine,' said Bilbo. He hummed 'Comin' Through the Rye' and smiled grimly to himself as he left the library.

FOURTEEN

'Mrs Rye?' The man on the step was short and wore a grey suit.

'*Doctor* Rye,' corrected Harper. 'How may I help you?'

The man fished in an inside pocket and flashed an ID card. 'Morton's my name, Doctor Rye. I'm with the Ministry of Defence. You released a pair of red kites in the Brecon Beacons last November, is that correct?'

'Yes.'

'And you claimed to have inherited the birds from

a Miss Olivia Wentworth of – let me see.' He unfolded a small square of paper. 'Of Waterside House, Walsham-le-Willows.'

'That is correct.'

'Well, no, Doctor Rye, that is *not* correct. There is no Waterside House at Walsham-le-Willows, and nobody seems to have heard of Miss Wentworth.'

'Oh,' murmured Harper.

Morton nodded. 'We thought perhaps you'd care to try again.'

'Try again?'

'Another story. The truth, perhaps.'

'The truth?' Harper smiled fleetingly. 'Very well, Mr Morton, you shall have it. The truth is that I have a time machine.'

Morton gazed at her coldly. 'This isn't a game, Doctor Rye. I'm here as a government representative with powers you probably wouldn't believe. If you persist in lying to me, you might well find yourself in a great deal of trouble. I'm going to give you one more chance to tell me the truth.'

Harper sighed. 'I've *told* you the truth, Mr Morton. I've got a time machine. It's in the house. If you'll follow me, I'll show it to you.'

'Rubbish!' snapped Morton. 'D'you think I'm an utter fool?' He gave Harper no time to answer but went on, 'Very well, if that's the way you want it

I'll bid you good-day, but I can assure you that you haven't heard the last of this — not by a long chalk.'

Harper watched from the step as the man spun on his heel and strode towards his chauffeur-driven car. 'Oh, dear,' she sighed.

FIFTEEN

Bilbo gazed at the printout. 'Four – the computer found four?'

The assistant nodded. 'One's the item from the *Gazette* – the one you showed me – but there are three others.'

'Great!' The boy's eyes gleamed behind the round lenses of his spectacles. 'How much do I owe you?'

'That'll be just two ecu, please.'

Bilbo paid, carried the printout to one of the study tables, and sat down. The first item was from something called the *Kettering Times*. It said:

Mr Trevor Sanderson of Market Harborough has caused a flutter among lepidopterists with his claim to have spotted a chequered skipper butterfly on a railway embankment near Bugbrooke. A spokesperson for the Northamptonshire Lepidoptery Association told our reporter, 'Mr Sanderson is almost certainly mistaken. The chequered skipper became extinct about twenty years ago.' In our picture, Mr Sanderson is pointing to the spot where he claims he saw the butterfly.

'Hmmm.' Bilbo moved on to the next piece, a three-liner from the *Merthyr Tydfil Advertiser*:

Police have arrested a man for allegedly shooting dead a red kite on M.o.D. land near Glyntawe. The red kite was thought to be extinct.

The last item had appeared in the *Princes Risborough Bugle*. It read:

Conservationists have mounted a round-the-clock vigil over a rare orchid found growing at an undisclosed location in the Chilterns. A spokesman would give no details, but said the orchid was of a type believed to have died out many years ago.

'So.' Bilbo sat back, took off his spectacles and

began polishing a lens with his handkerchief. 'Four examples. Three creatures and a plant, all thought to be extinct, all reappearing the same year. Coincidence?' He chuckled, replacing his glasses. 'No chance.'

He stood up, folded the printout and went back to the desk.

'Excuse me?' he said to the woman.

'Yes?'

'Could you find me the phone number of the *Sunday Sportsman*?'

The woman nodded. 'I think so.' She slid a fat volume towards her and flicked through it. 'Yes, here it is.' She read out the number. Bilbo wrote it on the back of the printout.

'Thanks.'

'You can phone from here, you know – there's a pay-phone in the foyer.'

Bilbo shook his head. 'I won't be phoning them just yet,' he smirked. 'I'm not quite ready.'

SIXTEEN

Jennifer Stone hated boys. They were loud and messy and rude. She was glad she and Kizzy had got through the holidays without Frazer wanting to tag along. So when she saw Andrew Baggins loitering as she took a shortcut through the churchyard on the day school started again, she groaned to herself. Andrew was the sort of boy who picked up worms and messed about with creepy-crawlies. You never knew what boys like Andrew might be hiding in their pockets.

'Hi, Jenny.' Bilbo's pale eyes weren't smiling. 'How was your stay with the Ryes?'

'It was good. Kizzy and I had a great time.' Why do you want to know? she wondered. And why are you blocking my way?

'See the newts, did you?'

'Newts?' Jennifer shivered. Is that what he's got in his pocket? 'No, I didn't, and I wouldn't want to.'

'Why not? Interesting creatures, newts. *I* saw 'em.'

'Good. Can I come past, please – it's ten to nine?'

Bilbo shook his head. 'Not yet. I want to ask you something first.'

'Well, hurry up then.' She wished someone would come by – a teacher perhaps – but nobody did.

'How long were you at their place?'

'Four nights.'

'Did you see or hear anything unusual at all?'

Jennifer shook her head. 'I don't think so.'

'You sure?' Bilbo's hand went to his jacket pocket. 'Seen a mole, have you? Close up? Dead?'

'Ugh!' Jennifer took a step backwards. 'No, I haven't. I'd be sick.'

'I've got one here, Jenny. It's gone stiff and it pongs a bit, but its coat's like velvet. It'd feel lovely sliding down the back of your neck. Are you absolutely certain nothing happened at Kizzy's?'

'Well—' Jennifer's eyes were on the boy's pocket.

'There *was* one thing. It was nothing, really. Just something Kizzy said when we were lying in the grass. She talks to herself sometimes.'

Bilbo came a step closer. His hand was in his pocket. Jennifer fancied she could smell the mole. 'What did she say, Jenny?'

'She said, "I wonder what our chequered skipper's doing at this moment?" I know it sounds stupid, but I thought she meant her dad. Her dad left, you know. I thought maybe he'd been a sailor or something and "our chequered skipper" was their pet name for him.'

Bilbo chuckled briefly. 'So what did *you* say?'

'I said, "pardon" or something like that, and she said, "nothing", sort of sharply, as if I was prying.'

'Then what?'

'Then she sat up and looked down at me and said, "Forget what I said just now, Jenny. If you're my friend, forget it." I didn't know what she was on about. I still don't.'

Bilbo smiled. 'Excellent. Do you know what a chequered skipper *really* is, Jenny?'

The girl nodded. 'It's a butterfly. I looked it up.'

'Right.' Bilbo removed his hand from his pocket. 'If you're my friend, Jennifer – mine and my mole's –

not a word to anyone about our little talk this morning. OK?'

Jennifer gulped and nodded. 'OK.'

'Fine.' Bilbo grinned and stepped aside. 'Off you go then – don't want to be late, do we, first morning back?'

SEVENTEEN

'Know what my dad reckons?' It was breaktime. Boys lolled about the bike sheds. Some smoked. Others, glassy-eyed and jiggling, were wired for sound. A few talked. Frazer looked at Stanton Sefton, who liked to be called SS.

'What does your dad reckon?' Frazer disliked Sefton and never called him SS. He didn't give a damn what the moron's dad reckoned, but talking passed the time.

'He reckons what this country needs is Hitler.'

'Oh, does he?' Frazer faked interest. 'He's the guy started World War Two, right?'

The other boy nodded.

'And gassed millions of people.'

'Yep.'

'So how come this country needs a guy like that?'

'Discipline, my dad says. Keep folk in line.'

Frazer nodded. 'Do what I say or be bumped off, you mean?'

'Right.'

'Sounds terrific. And I bet your dad'd volunteer to be commandant of one of the camps, wouldn't he – a death camp?'

Sefton nodded. 'That's exactly what he says. Here – how'd you know that, Rye?'

Frazer smiled. 'A guess, Sefton. A lucky guess.' He nodded and moved away, but for some reason he couldn't get Sefton's words out of his head.

EIGHTEEN

'Hello?' Andrew Baggins watched the teatime traffic through the clear plastic hood of the telephone kiosk. 'Is that the *Sunday Sportsman*?'

'Ye-es. How may I help you?'

'I'd like to speak to Harvey Parvin, please.'

'Is Mr Parvin expecting your call?'

'Not unless he's telepathic, but he'll want to hear what I have to tell him.'

'Yes, well – if you'll give me your name, I'll see if he's in.'

'Baggins. Andrew Baggins.'

'And how old are you, Mr Baggins?'

Bilbo sighed. 'Fifteen. How old are *you?*'

'Hold the line, please.'

There was a burst of rousing orchestral music, followed by a grunt. 'Parvin.'

'Oh, hi, Mr Parvin. My name's Baggins. Friends call me Bilbo. I've got a lead for you.'

'Is that right?' The journalist sounded less than thrilled. 'Go on then – what is it?'

'Do you – er – d'you pay for information, Mr Parvin?'

'Sometimes. Depends. Tell me what you've got.'

Bilbo hesitated. 'It's going to sound daft over the phone, Mr Parvin. Can't we meet? I've documents to show you.'

'Look, Mr Baggins, I'm a busy man. I can't just drop what I'm doing and rush out to meet some kid who says he's got a lead. You're going to have to *interest* me, son. Know what I mean?'

'Yes. Would a time machine interest you at all?'

There was a brief silence. It had begun to drizzle. Droplets beaded the hood, distorting Bilbo's view.

'Now listen, son. I told you I was busy. I don't have time for silly games. The *Sunday Sportsman*'s a newspaper, not a sci-fi mag, so if you don't mind I'm going to hang up now and get on with—'

'No!' cried Bilbo. 'Don't hang up. Listen, please.'

Speaking rapidly, he told the journalist what he'd seen at the Ryes' place, and about his discoveries since. When he'd finished there was another silence, broken only by the swish of tyres on wet tarmac. Then Parvin said, 'OK, son, it's just possible you've stumbled on something, though it sounds pretty far-fetched to me. D'you know the Hammer and Anvil at Long Melford?'

'The pub?'

'That's right. I'll meet you there at two o'clock tomorrow, OK?'

'I'll have to wag off school.'

The journalist chuckled. 'Even better then, isn't it?' He hung up.

NINETEEN

When farmer Stan Rickerby glanced out of the kitchen window that Tuesday morning, he expected to see what he always saw – forty Friesian cows dotted across the nine-acre meadow, chewing the cud and waiting to be milked. In fact, he was so certain he'd see this that he glanced and looked away, then uttered an exclamation and looked again.

The cows stood in a corner by the hedge, gazing at an enormous grey mound which occupied the middle of the field. For a moment, Stan thought someone must have come in the night and dumped ten truckloads of rubbish, but then the mound moved and his jaw dropped. 'It's— It looks like—' He knuckled his eyes, looked again and staggered to the phone.

'Hello – is that Janet?' Janet was married to the local bobby. 'Stan here, Janet. Stan Rickerby. Is John there? Yes, please.'

He stood jiggling the phone till the constable said, 'John here – what's the problem, Stan?'

'There's – I've just looked out and there's a whale in the nine acre.'

'A *what*?'

'A whale – or maybe it's a whacking gurt fish, I dunno.'

'Have you been at the scrumpy, Stan?'

'No, I haven't. It's there all right, whatever it is, and I want you to come out and take a look.'

'Have *you* had a look, Stan – a close one, I mean? How big's this thing?'

'I dunno, John. I only seen it through the window, but it's big – like three, four buses, I reckon. And it moved.'

The policeman sighed. 'OK, Stan, I'll be with you in ten minutes. Better stand clear till I get there.'

'Th-thanks, John.' The farmer's hand shook as he put down the phone. He muttered to himself and shook his head as he returned slowly to the window.

TWENTY

Breaktime round the bike sheds. Stanton Sefton laughs out loud, removing his headphones. 'Hey – anyone tuned local?'

Nobody is. Sefton laughs again. 'You'll never guess the latest newsflash.'

'Don't tell me,' growls Frazer. 'Hitler's been spotted at Orford, right?'

'Close, kid,' laughs Stanton. 'Try again.'

Frazer shakes his head. 'Can't be bothered, Stanton. Tell us.'

'They found a whale in the middle of a field at Westleton.'

A chorus of derision greets this announcement. Somebody snatches Sefton's 'phones and tries to listen in, while somebody else hacks at his shin with a trainer. Only Frazer is silent. He watches the developing mêlée for a moment, then turns and begins running towards the school building.

'Mum?'

'Frazer? Where are you? Is something wrong?'

'I'm calling from school, Mum. Nothing's wrong – at least, not here. Did you do the whale snatch last night?'

'Well, yes, darling, as a matter of fact I did, but I don't think we should be discussing it over the phone, and anyway how did you know?'

'You missed, Mum. Your whale's in a field at Westleton. It's on the news.'

TWENTY-ONE

'Yes, sir?' The landlord beamed at Bilbo across the bar of his almost empty lounge.

'Oh, I'm – I'm meeting somebody here. Two o'clock. Do you have Coke?'

'Certainly, sir. Ice and lemon?'

'Oh, yes please, that'll be great.'

'Take a seat and I'll bring it to you.'

Bilbo sat at a copper-top table with a green glass ashtray on it. The room's only other occupant – a very old man in a stained and shiny waistcoat – stared at him from a far corner. Bilbo avoided his gaze, pretending to study the sporting prints on the walls till his drink arrived.

'That'll be one fifteen, sir.'

'One—?'

Bilbo flushed, groping through his pockets, thinking, No wonder there's nobody here. He found the money, but it was a close thing.

'Thank you, sir.' The landlord waddled off. Bilbo sat gazing into the most expensive drink he'd ever bought. It was five to two.

'Mr Baggins?'

Bilbo, who'd been daydreaming, looked up with a start. 'Y-yes, that's me.'

'Harvey Parvin.' The man stuck out a hand. They shook briefly and Parvin sat down. He was a shortish, thickset man of about thirty-five with a dark, bushy moustache and a head of curly hair. He wore a black leather jacket and jeans. The landlord came over and the journalist ordered a pint of lager. He didn't speak till it had been delivered and he'd taken a long pull.

'So – what is it you've got to show me, son?'

Bilbo fished in an inside pocket. 'I know you think it's far-fetched,' he said, 'but—'

'No.' Parvin shook his head. 'No, I don't. Not any more. Not after what I've seen this morning. Show me.' Bilbo passed him the printout. Parvin unfolded it, smoothed it out and read rapidly, grunting and nodding at intervals. 'OK.' He gazed at Bilbo. 'I'd like to hang on to this. These people – the Ryes – I'll need their address.'

Bilbo gave it. Parvin wrote it down on a pad. Bilbo said, 'What *did* you see this morning?'

The journalist smiled. 'Only a whale, that's all. An extinct whale, alive, in the middle of a field two miles from the sea.'

Bilbo's eyes widened. 'Really? A whale? So what're you going to do next, Mr Parvin?'

Instead of answering the man said, 'Have you got a bank account, son?'

Bilbo shook his head. The journalist sighed, produced a fat wallet and counted out some notes which he folded and passed across the table. 'There you go – there's fifty E there. That's for the information you've given me, and for your discretion. Know what discretion means, do you?'

Bilbo shook his head and the man sighed again.

'Discretion means you don't tell anybody you've spoken to me, you don't give anybody else the information you've just sold to me – it's *mine* now – and you don't ask me what I'm going to do next. *That's* discretion.'

Bilbo nodded. 'I – I didn't do this just for the money, Mr Parvin. I wouldn't want you to think that. I did it because I believe scientists ought to—'

The man looked at him. 'I don't give a monkey's what you did it for, sunshine,' he growled. 'You've had my money, so as far as I'm concerned you're bought and paid for. Finish your drink, stand up and walk out. Don't say anything, don't look back, and don't come near this pub again till you're eighteen. Cheers.' He lifted his glass and drank deeply and, when he put it down, Bilbo had gone.

TWENTY-TWO

Harper Rye tuned into Heartbeat when her son rang off and stayed tuned all day. Every hour the station broadcast a news bulletin, and today each bulletin was an update on the whale story. Early updates just called it a whale, but later, as experts began arriving on the scene, it became a sperm whale, a female sperm whale, and a female sperm whale long thought to be extinct. Harper fretted, wondering how long it would be before the national media picked up the story.

She didn't know what to do. She wished she could snatch the whale again – make it vanish from the meadow at Westleton and drop it in the sea off Dunwich where its mate was presumably waiting, but Rye's Apparatus wasn't geared to snatch things from the present. She could only sit tight, listening to the updates, hoping somebody would come up with an explanation as to how the creature might have got where it was – an explanation which didn't involve a time machine, and which people would accept.

There were plenty of theories. One man thought there must have been a freak tidal wave during the night – a wave which swept four kilometres inland and left the creature stranded. Another said the whole thing would probably turn out to be a student prank or a publicity stunt to advertise washing powder. It was a sign from God, a mass hallucination and a message from outer space. From the depth of her distress, Harper found time to marvel at the number and variety of screwballs in our midst. It consoled her to learn that concerned, sensible people were at the scene too. The whale was still alive, and teams from Greenpeace and the Whale and Dolphin Conservation Society were involved in what was described as a race against time to devise a way of getting the creature into the sea.

At three o'clock it was time to go for Frazer and Kizzy. Harper walked out to the Suzuki. All seemed normal, which probably meant nobody linked the whale incident to her. It's only a matter of time though, she told herself gloomily, remembering Morton of the M.o.D. She climbed in and started the engine. As the Suzuki swung out of the driveway, its nearside door brushed the shrub behind which Harvey Parvin was crouching.

TWENTY-THREE

He worked his way round the outside of the house, trying doors and looking in windows. The doors were all locked and the windows he could see through revealed only the sorts of things you'd expect to find in a house. There was a wing whose windows were covered by pull-down blinds, which was frustrating. He considered breaking in, but decided to check the outbuildings first. Like Bilbo before him, he opened doors and peered through dark windows, but found nothing of interest. He was examining the lock on the kitchen door when he heard the Suzuki returning.

He crossed the yard, slipped into an outhouse and pulled the door closed behind him.

'So what do we *do*, Mum?' asked Frazer as the three of them entered the house.

Harper shrugged. 'I don't know, darling. We can't run away – the apparatus isn't portable. We *could* lock ourselves in and refuse to answer the door, but I don't fancy our chances against the M.o.D. No.' She threw the keys on the table and switched on the radio. 'We'll just have to wait. Carry on the good work and hope nobody connects that poor old whale with us.'

There was good news on the five o'clock bulletin. Using a low loader and keeping the whale wet with bedsheets and buckets of water, Greenpeace and the Whale and Dolphin Conservation Society had succeeded in getting the creature to the sea. It was in the sea now, off Dunwich. Heartbeat's reporter-on-the-spot could see it clearly from where she was standing. It didn't seem to be doing much, she told her listeners – lying on the surface two hundred metres beyond the surf, shaken perhaps by its ordeal but definitely alive.

'Well,' smiled Kizzy as Harper switched off. 'That's *something*, I suppose.'

Dinner was a subdued affair. When it was over Kizzy said, 'It's Frazer's turn to wash up, Mum. I'm off biking.'

Harper looked at her. 'Be careful, darling. Watch the traffic, don't talk to anyone and be home well before dark.'

'Aw, *Mum!*' sighed Kizzy. 'I *know*. I'm not a baby, for goodness sake.'

'You're *my* baby,' smiled Harper. 'You always will be, so you might as well get used to it.'

Kizzy crossed the yard to the outbuilding where she kept her bike. Harvey Parvin saw her coming and got down behind a mildewed sofa. He'd just had an idea and it was making him smile.

TWENTY-FOUR

Kizzy heard the car behind her and pulled over to the left. 'Come on then,' she murmured, accustomed to the impatience of drivers. 'Pass me – I'm not stopping you.' She was a mile from the village, in a place where the road passed through dense woodland. Trees overhung the lane on either side, shutting out the sun, forming a dim green tunnel which made Kizzy imagine she was cycling underwater.

The car was close behind now, going at a crawl, making no effort to overtake. Kizzy glanced back. It was a blue Mazda. The man behind the wheel seemed to be smiling. Some words of her mother's came into her head. Funny men. Never get in anybody's car, Harper had said. There are funny men about. Mum called them funny, but Kizzy knew that the sort of men she was talking about weren't funny at all. They were scary. They liked to hurt children, or even kill them. She put on a spurt, pedalling as fast as she could. The driver accelerated to stay close behind. Oh Lord, breathed Kizzy. What now? What shall I *do*?

Stop, said a voice in her head. If you stop he'll have to pass. She pulled over and stopped, propped on her left leg, listening, praying that the car would go by.

It didn't. It came scrunching up and stopped beside her. The nearside window was down. The driver leaned across, smiling. He had a moustache and curly hair. He reminded Kizzy of someone she'd seen on the telly. 'Hello,' he said. His eyes twinkled. 'You're Kizzy, aren't you?'

Kizzy was startled. How did he know her name? She was sure she'd never seen him before. Instead of replying she set off again, standing on the pedals, wobbling. The car rolled forward, staying level. Kizzy stopped. The car stopped too. The driver was laughing. 'Don't keep running away,' he said. 'I only want to talk to you.'

'What about?' Kizzy was tense. If he opens his door I'm off, she thought.

'Get in the car.'

'Get lost — d'you think I'm stupid or something? My mum's told me about men like you.'

The man chuckled. 'Funny men, you mean?'

Kizzy flushed. 'How did *you* know?'

'Your mum's right, sweetheart. They're everywhere, but I'm not one of them. I chase information, not little girls. I think you've got some information for me, Kizzy.'

Kizzy shook her head. 'I don't think so.'

'Oh yes you have, sweetheart. I know you have. A little bird told me.'

'What bird?'

'The lesser-spotted Bilbo bird. You know the Bilbo bird, don't you?'

Kizzy nodded. 'So *that's* how you knew my name. Yes, I know Bilbo. He's a creepazoid, like you.'

'Now, now!' The man wagged a stubby finger, jokily severe. 'There's no need to be abusive, young woman. Tell me about your mum's machine.'

'Machine?' Kizzy frowned. 'I don't know what you mean. Mum hasn't got a machine, unless you mean the washing machine.'

He shook his head. 'I don't mean the washing machine, Kizzy. I mean the newt machine. The red kite machine. The whale machine.' He leaned closer. He wasn't smiling now. 'What I'm talking about is the *time* machine, sweetheart. Tell me about that.'

'No.' Kizzy shook her head. 'I don't know what you mean. I have to go home now.'

'You'll go home,' purred the man, 'just as soon as you give me the information.'

'And if I don't – what then?'

'Ah, well – then I just might have to turn into one of those funny men your mum warned you about.'

Fear washed over Kizzy, making her tremble. This was a lonely spot. Nobody had passed by while they'd been speaking. All the man had to do was bundle her into the car and drive off and nobody would ever see her again. They'd find her bike on the verge. Nothing else. She was helpless.

'All right,' she murmured. 'Promise you'll let me go and I'll tell you.'

'Now that's *much* better, sweetheart.' The smile was back. 'I'm right, aren't I – there *is* a machine?'

'Well—' As Kizzy opened her mouth, a girl of about her own age appeared round a bend and came pedalling towards them. Kizzy gasped with relief as she recognized Gabrielle Kromer, a classmate who lived in the neighbouring village of Elmswell.

'Gabrielle!' She called and waved. The other girl waved back and began to slow down. The man muttered something very rude and revved his engine. As Gabrielle steered her bike towards Kizzy, the Mazda shot forward in a cloud of blue exhaust and roared off round the bend.

'Who was that?' Gabrielle pulled up and gazed after the car.

'Oh, nobody,' smiled Kizzy. 'Just some guy wanting information.'

'Oh.' Gabrielle nodded. 'A tourist.'

'Something like that,' said Kizzy.

TWENTY-FIVE

'A man?' Harper's eyes widened. 'What man, darling – what did he want?'

Kizzy peeled off her jacket. 'I didn't know him, Mum. He was old – older than you, with a moustache and curly hair. He wanted information about the apparatus.'

'Did he *call* it that – the apparatus?'

'No, he called it a machine. Your mum's machine, he said.'

'But how did he know *you*, darling?'

Kizzy pulled a face. 'He'd talked to Andrew Baggins.'

'Bilbo? But what could Bilbo have told him, Kizzy?'

Kizzy shrugged. 'I dunno, Mum. The guy mentioned newts and red kites and whales. I don't see how Baggins could know about any of that, but he must've told him about me and given this address.'

Frazer walked into the room. 'What's the dreaded Bilbo been up to now?' he asked. Kizzy told him.

'Well, the rotten little plonker! You wait till I get my hands on him tomorrow.'

Harper shook her head. 'That's not going to help, Frazer. The damage is already done.'

'I bet he got money,' growled Frazer. 'He'd kill for money, that Bilbo. He's always been a miser.'

Harper looked at Kizzy. 'What did you tell the man, darling?'

'Nothing. I was going to, though – he scared me – but then Gabrielle showed up and he drove off.'

'Gabrielle?'

'Gabrielle Kromer from school.'

'Well, thank goodness for Gabrielle, that's all I can say.' Harper gave her daughter a hug. 'I'm afraid you'll have to stop biking off by yourself, darling – my nerves won't stand it.'

'Aw, Mu-um.'

'So who d'you reckon this guy was?' asked Frazer.

His mother shrugged. 'I don't know. Could be M.o.D. Could be the Press. Could be anybody. If I had to guess, I'd say he's a journalist on one of the tabloids. They'll stoop to anything to get what they want. We'll probably be headline news tomorrow.'

'But Kizzy didn't tell him anything,' cried Frazer.

Harper shook her head. 'From what he told Kizzy, it seems he's got half the story already. If he's like most of his colleagues he'll invent the rest.'

'So what do we *do*?'

Harper smiled grimly. 'We beat him to it, my darlings. Spoil his nice little exclusive.'

Kizzy frowned. 'How, Mum?'

'Simple. We contact the Press. Tell 'em everything.'

Frazer gazed at her. 'And then?'

His mother shook her head. 'Who knows?' she said.

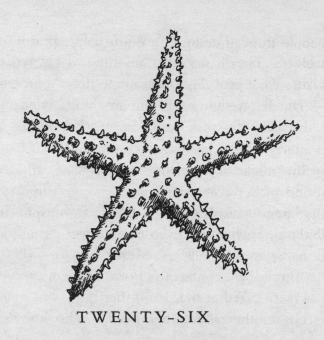

TWENTY-SIX

It was awful. More awful than any of them had dreamed it could be. Harper Rye faxed her hastily drafted press release to the national dailies at nine o'clock that Tuesday evening, and by half-past ten their home was under siege. The driveway became totally blocked with vehicles out of which poured reporters, photographers and TV crews, clogging the yard and garden, lugging their paraphernalia from place to place as they jostled for positions near doors and windows. Luckily, the Ryes had locked up and drawn all the curtains before anybody arrived, but this didn't prevent people from pounding on doors, rapping at windows and shouting through the letterbox. At eleven-thirty, Harper, hoarse from shouting 'go away' and seething with anger, flung open an upstairs window and yelled, 'For God's sake stop this insane racket and get off my property – my kids have school tomorrow.'

She might as well have saved her breath. At the sound of her voice there was a frantic surge towards the open window. Cameras flashed. Microphones like fluffy toys on sticks swayed at sill-height and somebody bellowed, 'Talk to us, Doctor Rye – the public has the right to know the truth.'

'Truth?' croaked Harper. 'Half of you wouldn't recognize the truth if it came up and smacked you in the teeth.' She slammed the window, picked up the bedroom extension and called the police.

It was one a.m. before local police, reinforced by officers from Bury St Edmunds, were able to persuade the invaders to depart and let the Ryes get some sleep. Even then, most of them didn't go far. Every room at every inn for kilometres around was occupied by journalists, and some of those who failed to find accommodation slept in their vehicles, so that when Kizzy peeped out at eight after a restless night, there were men on the lawn.

TWENTY-SEVEN

'No school today, my darlings,' smiled Harper as her dazed children trailed down to breakfast. 'Can't have you running the gauntlet of those vultures out there, and anyway it's ten past eight now – we'd never make it.'

'I'm glad,' yawned Frazer. 'I didn't fancy facing everybody today – people at school, I mean. Not if we're in the papers.'

Kizzy shook her head. 'Me neither. I've been thinking about that man. He might be after me again because we spoiled his story.'

They were halfway through breakfast when the phone rang. 'Oh, no,' groaned Harper. 'This makes four times this morning.' She got up. Kizzy expected her to start yelling at the caller but instead she sighed and relaxed against the wall, smiling. 'Oh, it's *you*, Hazel. Thank goodness. I thought – yes, yes, it's me all right. Us, I should say. We're besieged, my love. Trapped in our own home. What're they saying about us, anyway? Oh yes, I can imagine. Well – that's very kind, Hazel, and it'd be lovely to see you, but I wouldn't if I were you. You'd be mobbed – dragged from your vehicle and scragged before you could say "no comment". Well, if you're absolutely sure— You're a hero, darling, I've always said so. We'll keep the coffee on and man the door. Yes. Yes, we look forward to that. 'Bye.'

'Hazel's coming,' stated Frazer as his mother sat down.

Harper nodded. 'She is, the intrepid fool, *and* she's bringing the morning papers which are absolutely black with inaccurate headlines about us. We must be ready to let her in the instant she arrives.'

Hazel Ratcliffe lived and worked in Ipswich, and it was after ten when her Euro came bouncing up the driveway, pursued by four men on foot. As the car pulled up by the front door, Frazer flung it open and yelled, 'This way, Hazel – quick!'

It was a desperately close thing. As the lecturer scuttled into the hallway with a wodge of newspapers under her arm, a camera flashed. Frazer was momentarily blinded, and when he went to slam the door there was a foot in it. *'Aaaagh!'* The reporter screamed, snatched back his crushed foot and hopped about on the step, nursing it. When Frazer slammed the door it hit him a terrific blow on the ear. He toppled, rolled down the steps and lay sobbing at the feet of his slower colleagues. Kizzy, who had watched the whole thing through a curtained window, laughed maliciously and let the curtain fall.

TWENTY-EIGHT

'So let's have a look at what they're saying.' Harper slid a tabloid from the top of the pile while Hazel sipped coffee. Kizzy and Frazer peered at the headline over their mother's shoulder.

'DOCTOR WHO?' it bellowed.

'Oh, no,' groaned Harper for the second time that morning. She skimmed the story, threw the paper aside and reached for another.

'SUFFOLK MUM CLAIMS TARDIS BREAK-THROUGH!' it read. 'Copycat!' scoffed Harper.

'How about this?' Frazer grabbed a tabloid and read out: 'SUFFOLK HUNCH: BOFFIN'S TIME BREAKTHROUGH.'

'Oh, Lord!' sighed Harper. 'What an *excruciating* pun. Let's have another, quick.' She snatched one from the pile.

'SINGLE MUM IN CETACEAN RELOCATION SENSATION,' this one read, over a picture of the unfortunate whale. Harper laughed.

'Really imaginative effort from the *Financial Times*,' chuckled Hazel, pouring more coffee. 'TIME-TRAVEL CLAIM – MARKETS CAUTIOUS.'

Kizzy picked up a broadsheet. 'This one's different, Mum. It sounds foreign. Listen. KRA S'HAON SM.'

'Eh?' Frazer peered at the headline. 'KRA S'HAON SM? What the heck does that mean, Mum?'

Harper took the paper from Kizzy and studied the headline, frowning. Then her brow cleared and she chuckled. 'That's quite clever, I suppose. Try it backwards, darling.'

Kizzy's lips moved as she read the headline from right to left. A smile dawned. 'MS NOAH'S ARK,' she murmured. 'It *is* good, isn't it, in a way?'

'*I* don't think so,' growled Frazer. 'How many

people're going to try it backwards? They'll think it's gobbledygook.'

His mother shook her head. 'I doubt it, darling. That paper's famous for its crossword. I fancy most of its readers will spot the reversal pretty quickly. After all, it's only an anagram.'

'Well.' Hazel put down her cup and smiled. 'How does it feel to hit the headlines, folks?'

Harper grimaced. 'It's not the headlines that worry me, Hazel, it's the stories underneath. So much sensation, so few facts. I'm afraid—'

'Hey, Mum.' Kizzy was by the window. 'They're all going away – look.'

It was true. The yard was emptying. Only a three-man camera crew remained, dismantling its equipment. Frazer ran to the living-room, peered into the garden and yelled, 'It's the same this side, Mum. They're going.'

'Hooray!' cried Kizzy. 'We're free. We can go anywhere we like. Hey, Mum – Hazel – how about a picnic in the woods to celebrate?'

'Good idea,' laughed Hazel, but Harper didn't respond. She was gazing through the window at a man standing in the gateway. She was sure she'd seen him before. He was watching the cars and vans depart. When the last one had gone, he turned to look at the

91

house and she remembered who he was. 'Mr Morton,' she murmured.

'What?' queried Kizzy.

'Mr Morton's here,' said Harper. 'Morton of the M.o.D. I think our picnic might have to wait a while.'

TWENTY-NINE

'This press release,' said Morton, when he and Harper were alone in the living-room. 'Is there any truth in it?'

Harper gazed at him. 'Of course. I told you when you came before but you refused to listen. How did you get rid of the media?'

'I'll ask the questions if you don't mind, Doctor Rye. So that's how you got hold of those red kites – with your time machine?'

Harper nodded. 'I prefer to call it Rye's Apparatus, Mr Morton. Time machine sounds so sci-fi, don't you think?'

The man shrugged. 'The name is immaterial, Doctor Rye. The point is that if your claim is true, you have invented a device with immense potential and to go to the Press the way you did was an act of gross irresponsibility. Foreign powers will have been alerted. They may well wish to possess your – apparatus. Did that possibility not occur to you?'

Harper nodded. 'Mr Morton, I am well aware that there are unscrupulous people who will use any new invention for their own ends, but it was a risk I had to take for the sake of my children. We were being hounded by the tabloids. As far as I'm concerned, my apparatus is a device for reintroducing to the Earth plants and animals which we have wiped out with our thoughtlessness and our greed. Used responsibly, it can only be a good thing. It is *not* a weapon.'

Morton frowned. 'Unfortunately, Doctor, that is not for you to decide. If your apparatus has military potential, your country will want to exploit it. It's as simple as that.' He stood up. 'Show it to me.'

Suppressing her anger, the physicist led Morton to the room at the end of the house which served as her laboratory. She unlocked the door and stood aside to let him enter. 'There. That's my apparatus.'

Morton gazed at the gleaming ring of micro-circuitry in the middle of the room. 'Good Lord,' he breathed. 'And it really works, eh?'

Harper made no reply. She was trying to imagine how this man and those like him might twist her invention into a killing machine. There was no doubt in her mind that they'd manage it.

'And what's that?' Morton nodded towards the console which occupied all of one wall.

'That's my control centre,' said Harper. 'It's basically a linked series of computers. Would you like me to demonstrate?'

He looked at her. 'Capture something from the past, you mean? Bring it here, now?'

Harper nodded. 'That's what it does.'

He hesitated, drawing his tongue along his lower lip. Then, reluctantly it seemed, he shook his head. 'No – that won't be necessary, thank you.' He cleared his throat. 'Soon, our people will come and remove this apparatus to one of our evaluation centres. At that stage you may well be required to demonstrate, and to advise. In the meantime I would urge you to keep the device, together with any papers pertaining to it, totally—'

'Hey, just a minute!' cried Harper. 'This is *my* apparatus you're talking about. It's *mine*. How d'you mean, *our people will come and remove it*? You can't just—'

Morton stared at her, unblinking. 'Oh, but we can, Doctor Rye. I promise you, we can.'

'What about the Press, then? *They'll* be back the minute you leave, wanting to know—'

Morton shook his head. 'The Press won't bother you again.' He smiled a brief, tight smile. 'That's another promise.'

He didn't stay for the coffee Harper offered, and she was glad. She'd offered it out of politeness, but it had felt like offering hospitality to a burglar. When he'd gone, and Hazel asked if she was feeling all right, she surprised herself by flinging her arms round her friend and bursting into tears.

THIRTY

'Do we *have* to go today, Mum – can't we wait till Monday?' Kizzy had on her best pleading look, but Harper was adamant.

'You have to get it over with, darling, and it would feel just as difficult on Monday as it does today.' She smiled. 'Anyway, it won't be half as bad as you think it's going to be – things never are.'

'Huh – you don't know the kids, Mum. They'll be there already, waiting to pounce.'

'Yeah,' nodded Frazer. 'At my place, too. That Sefton.'

All arguments proved futile. At eight o'clock, brother and sister were in the Suzuki with their bags between their feet, and Harper was steering the vehicle out of the driveway.

She dropped them at around eight-thirty and set off back, unsure of what her next move ought to be. There was the white-headed duck, of course – a recently extinct bird she'd intended snatching from the nineteen nineties – but Morton and the Press had unsettled her. Especially Morton, whom she found sinister in spite of his grey suit and quiet way of speaking. Or perhaps *because* of them.

She was thinking about Morton as she swung the Suzuki on to the rough track which led to the house, and she didn't notice the girl till it was almost too late. She gasped and stood on the brake, bringing the vehicle to a screeching halt. The girl stood in the middle of the track, gazing in at her as though nothing had happened. Harper, shaken and furious, wound down her window.

'What the devil do you think you're doing?' she snapped. 'Do you realize I almost killed you just now?'

The girl smiled dreamily. 'That would've been all right – I'd be with *him*, you see – for ever.' As the girl spoke, two others emerged from the shrubs and stood behind her, and Harper noticed they all wore the same T-shirts.

'What are you talking about, you silly girl? You don't *want* to die, surely?'

The girl shook her head. 'Not if *he* can live again.'

'He?' cried Harper. 'Who's this *he* you keep mentioning?'

The girl smiled again. 'Vulcan Pan, of course. The most fantastic guy who ever lived. He was God, you know.'

'Vulcan—? Ah, right.' Harper nodded. Vulcan Pan, the pop star. Frazer had been keen on him a couple of years back. She looked at the girl. 'But he's – he's dead, isn't he? A car crash or something.'

The girl shook her head. 'Not to us, he's not. Look.' She opened her jacket to reveal the words on her T-shirt. VULCAN PAN LIVES. She gazed at the physicist with shining eyes. 'We stayed faithful, you see, and now we know why. We were chosen – *he* chose us to come to you and fix his resurrection.'

'Fix his— Oh, no.' Harper shook her head. 'No, no, no. No, you've made a mistake, my dear, believe me. I can't – it's impossible, that's all. Quite impossible.'

'Oh no, it's not.' The girl's eyes filled with tears. 'Don't say that to us. Not to *us*. We stayed faithful all this time, and it was for *this*. It was for *you*. We were waiting – *he* was waiting – for you. Don't you *see*?'

Harper shook her head. She felt sick. The Suzuki's engine had stalled when she braked. She restarted it and called over its growl, 'Go away, please. I really am most terribly sorry, but I can't help you and you must leave. This is a private track and you're trespassing.' She released the brake and the Suzuki rolled forward. At the last possible moment the girls stepped aside, their faces streaked with tears. Harper kept her gaze fixed straight ahead but she could feel their eyes on her, and when she drew level, the girl who had spoken spat through the open window and cried, 'We *won't* leave, d'you hear? We'll *camp* here till you change your mind. *He'll* come to you. *He'll* make you do what we want!'

Harper drove on, wiping spittle from her cheek with the back of her hand.

THIRTY-ONE

'Look out, guys – here comes Doctor Who!' Ashley Hallas pointed as Frazer walked into the yard. Kids, yelling and cheering, converged on their victim so that he found himself in the middle of a jostling scrum.

'Hey, Rye!' shouted someone. 'Get us a whale.'

'Yeah!' cried another. 'Dump it in the assembly hall – close the school.'

'What about a Bengal tiger for the Head's bedroom?' suggested a girl.

'And a fistful of newts in old Ibbotson's knickers!'

demanded another. Ms Ibbotson taught Biology.

'OK, OK,' grinned Frazer. 'I knew it was going to be like this. All suggestions will be given careful consideration, as the Chairman of Governors might say, but I'm making no promises.' Ironic cheers greeted this pronouncement. Frazer surveyed the crowd. 'Anybody seen Bilbo this morning?'

'I have,' volunteered Hallas. 'Shall I tell him a Time Lord wants to see him?'

'Tell him nothing,' growled Frazer. 'Where is he?'

'He *was* skulking behind the toolshed, scoffing a choc bar. Someone seems to have left him a million E or something – he's spending it like water these days.'

Andrew Baggins was stuffing the remains of a Snickers bar into his face when Frazer found him. He didn't seem pleased to see his friend.

'Whaddya want?' he grunted, through a cud of sugary goo.

'Nothing *you've* got, you rotten little plonker,' snarled Frazer. 'You were a guest in our home and you spied on us.'

'Howdya mean?' Brown spit oozed from a corner of Bilbo's mouth and trickled down his chin.

'You went snooping around the place, trying to find out about my mother's work even though I told you it was hush-hush, and then you spilled your guts to some media-creep who threatened my sister and forced Mum to go public.' He grabbed a handful of the boy's shirt and tie. 'How much did he pay you, Baggins?'

'N-nothing,' spluttered Bilbo. 'Honest.'

'Did it for love, did you?'

'Yes. I mean, no. It was scientific enquiry, Frazer. People have a right to know.'

'Right to know, you sanctimonious little twerp?' Frazer tightened his grip and lifted Bilbo off his feet. The boy's face reddened and his eyes goggled as Frazer's fist closed his airway. He gasped, dribbling liquified Snickers down his face. Frazer used his free hand to scrape up a palmful of the mess, which he then proceeded to smear over every part of Bilbo's face and into his ears. He ended by rubbing the stuff vigorously into the boy's hair before letting him fall to the ground, where he lay sniffling.

Frazer was washing his hands in the cloakroom when the buzzer signalled the start of the school day and Stanton Sefton sidled up to him. 'Hey, Rye,' he murmured. 'Your mum picks you up after school, right?'

'Right.'

'Well, my dad wants to talk to her. He'll be by the gate at half-past three.'

'OK. I'm not sure she'll talk to him, though.'

Sefton chuckled nastily and ruffled Frazer's hair. 'Oh, she'll talk to him all right, kiddo,' he said. 'People usually do what my dad wants.' He walked on.

Frazer gazed after him. He'd felt good after his session with Bilbo, but he didn't feel so good now.

THIRTY-TWO

A ring of children held hands and danced round Kizzy, chanting, 'a panda, a panda, a panda!'

'I can't. It isn't *like* that. Mum's not in the *pets* trade. Her animals are for releasing into the wild.' Her words were disregarded – drowned out by the chanting. She wished the bell would go.

'Leave her alone!'

Kizzy's heart soared as Jennifer Stone appeared, fighting to break the circle, tugging it out of shape as she hauled on a boy's arm. Kizzy charged the same boy who, finding himself under attack from front and rear, relinquished his grip on his friends' hands and whirled, ready to defend himself. As he did so, Gabrielle Kromer arrived, flinging herself at the girl next to him. The circle disintegrated as its members, out for fun but not for a fight, scattered. In a moment the three girls found themselves in possession of this bit of the playground.

'Thanks,' breathed Kizzy. 'That chanting was starting to do my head in.'

'Any time,' grinned Gabrielle. 'Nothing like a good scrap to set you up for the day, is there, Jenny?'

Jennifer, who hated fighting, smiled and looked down. The three friends drifted towards the building in anticipation of the bell.

At the end of assembly Mr Donovan said, 'I want to see Kizzy Rye in my room right away, please.'

Kizzy swallowed. Kids were whispering – turning round to look at her. She felt her cheeks going red.

'Now, Kizzy.' The Head gazed at her across his desk. 'I noticed a disturbance in the playground this morning. You seemed to be in the middle of it. What was it all about?'

'Sir, they—'

'Never mind *they*. What were *you* doing?'

'I – I was trying to tell them, sir.'

'Tell them what?'

'That my mother can't get them a panda, sir.'

'A panda? What on earth are you talking about, Kizzy Rye?'

'Sir, they think I can get them a panda with my mother's apparatus. I was trying to explain—'

'Ah, yes.' Mr Donovan nodded. 'Your mother's apparatus. Now we're coming to it.'

'Pardon, sir?'

'I said we were coming to it, Kizzy. The heart of the matter. I read the papers too, you know.'

'Yes, sir.'

'Yes, sir.' He nodded, regarding Kizzy from beneath his bushy eyebrows. 'Fame, Kizzy. Or notoriety. Mustn't get carried away by it must we, hmm? Mustn't let it go to our heads.'

'Sir, I'm *not*. I—'

'Don't *interrupt*, child. Don't *contradict*. Listen. I know you, Kizzy, as I know every child in my school. I watch you, you see. You've always been a quiet child. A good child. A hard worker who never makes a fuss. Then your mother gets her name in the papers and in no time at all you're causing disruption in the playground. It won't do, Kizzy, do you understand? I won't have it.'

'But, sir, I— It's not fair. I didn't start it. They were all waiting for me.'

107

'That will do, Kizzy. I'm not interested in excuses. Just remember what I've said. We don't have prima donnas at this school.'

'There's *one*.' She hadn't meant to say it. She was angry and it just slipped out. The Head's gaze was chilling.

'*What* did you say, Kizzy Rye?'

'Nothing, sir.'

'It didn't sound like nothing to me.' He stood up. 'I'm disappointed in you, Kizzy. Bitterly disappointed. I shall write to your mother. Go to your class now.'

Kizzy went to her class, but she did no work. She couldn't. Her mind kept going over the terrible thing she'd said to Mr Donovan – the letter her mother would get. 'I wish,' she whispered, over and over, 'I wish I'd never *heard* of Rye's Apparatus.'

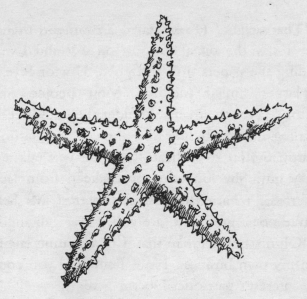

THIRTY-THREE

Harper lowered the Suzuki's window to watch the kids streaming through the gateway. She'd just spotted Frazer when a shadow fell across her and a man poked his head in.

'It's Doctor Rye, isn't it?'

'Yes.' Harper's tone was cautious. 'And this is my daughter, Kizzy.'

The man nodded. 'Hello, Kizzy.' He smiled briefly then looked at Harper. 'My name's Martin Sefton. My son's in Frazer's year.'

'Oh, yes. Frazer's mentioned him. Stanton, isn't it?'

'That's right.' He hesitated a moment, then went on. 'I saw the bit about you on TV and I've been reading the papers. I'm intrigued, Doctor Rye.'

Harper smiled ruefully. 'Most people are, Mr Sefton.' Over the man's shoulder she could see Frazer twirling a finger beside his temple then pointing it at Martin Sefton to indicate that she was talking to a crazy guy. She looked away to keep from laughing and said, 'What exactly is your interest, Mr Sefton – you're not a journalist, are you?'

'Oh no, nothing like that. I'm a heating engineer – run my own business. No – I suppose you could say my interest's patriotic, Doctor Rye.'

'Patriotic?'

'Yes. Things haven't been going too well with the old country lately, have they? Recession, violent crime, bombings, riots. People aren't safe on the streets any more.'

Harper nodded. 'True.'

'Ever wondered why?'

'I *know* why, Mr Sefton. There are no decent jobs. People are homeless. Conditions like these are bound to cause unrest.'

'No, no, Doctor.' The man shook his head vigorously. 'All that is incidental. What's wrong – what's *missing* – is strong leadership.'

'You think so?'

'I *know* so. What this country needs is a leader who sees what needs to be done and does it, no matter how unpopular it makes him. A man who doesn't *care* what people think.'

Harper shook her head. 'That doesn't sound like a very good idea to me, Mr Sefton. What you're describing is some sort of dictator, and anyway I don't see what all this has to do with my work, so if you'll excuse me I have to get my kids home.'

Sefton shook his head. 'Not *some sort* of dictator, Doctor Rye. I'm not talking about *some sort* of dictator. I'm talking about *the* dictator – the greatest man who ever lived. I'm talking about Adolf Hitler.'

'*Hitler?*' Harper laughed. 'You're insane, Mr Sefton. Adolf Hitler was responsible for more suffering than any single man before or since. He was nothing but a monster.' She peered over Sefton's shoulder and called, 'Frazer? Come along, darling – time to go.'

'Wait!' As she started the engine the man reached in and grabbed the wheel. 'We can bring him back. You and I. Bring him *here*. With his methods and the backing of the organization I belong to, he'd *transform* this country – turn it around. And it would all be down to you, Doctor Rye – you and your wonderful machine!'

Harper looked at the man. 'What exactly *is* this organization of yours, Mr Sefton?'

The man's smile was wolfish. 'The New Britain Movement, naturally. They're the only true patriots we have left in this country.'

'They're Nazis,' snarled Harper. 'A bunch of Nazi thugs who can't muster a decent brain between them. Take your hand off my wheel, please – we're going.'

Frazer was clambering into the Suzuki. Sefton retained his grip. 'Listen,' he hissed. 'The NBM will do anything for England, Doctor Rye – *anything*.' He was forced to let go of the wheel as the Suzuki rolled forward. 'You'll get a visit from us one of these nights – you can depend on it. Nobody says no to me.'

'I *told* you he was nuts,' chuckled Frazer as they pulled away. 'It runs in the family.'

'It's not *funny*!' cried Kizzy. 'I got in trouble today because of all this and it wasn't my fault. I wish we could just go away and forget all about it.'

'I'm sorry,' sighed Harper. 'Really I am.' She was thinking about the pop fans waiting by the gateway at home. 'I'll get us out of this, darlings, I promise. Somehow, I'll get us out.'

She wished she felt as confident as she sounded.

THIRTY-FOUR

The fans were waiting. They'd constructed a bender – a shelter made from saplings and polythene – among the shrubs just outside the gateway. As the Suzuki came bouncing down the track, they emerged from this and linked arms, blocking the way. There were five of them now.

'What the heck's *this*?' cried Frazer.

'Sorry, darlings,' muttered Harper, hitting the brake and the horn at the same time. 'It's the Vulcan Pan fan club. They want me to snatch their hero – resurrect him, as they put it.'

'I don't believe it.'

As the vehicle squealed to a stop, the young women broke their chain and surrounded it, rapping on windows, pressing their faces against the glass, chanting. One girl leant across the bonnet and held a sheet of paper to the windscreen. On it, in green felt-tip, were the words:

YOUR DESTINY YOU CAN'T DENY –
BRING BACK OUR VULCAN, DOCTOR
RYE

'My God,' breathed Frazer. 'They're even nuttier than Martin Sefton. What're you going to *do*, Mum?'

'Creep forward, I suppose,' said Harper. 'Very slowly, and hope they don't attack with stones or something.' She blipped the horn and eased the Suzuki forward at five kilometres an hour. The fans kept pace, pounding on the roof with their fists and pulling such hideous faces that Kizzy closed her eyes. As the vehicle began to pass between the gateposts, they fell away and stood in a sullen knot, watching it recede. There were no stones, and no more spittle.

'Are we getting the police?' asked Frazer, as his mother drew up by the door. 'They'll soon shift 'em.'

Harper shook her head. 'I don't think so, dear. They're seriously mixed up but I doubt if they're dangerous. It's that Sefton character *I'm* worried about.'

The fans chanted steadily through the evening, forcing the Ryes to keep the windows closed and drown them out with TV. It was after ten when the noise finally stopped and the two youngsters went to bed. Harper switched off the television and sat in the dark, wrestling with the problem of what to do. Used as she'd intended, Rye's Apparatus was harmless. In fact, it was positively beneficial, yet already there were people out there who wanted it used in other ways – to alter human history and to hurt others. Some of them were crazy, of course, and they could probably be coped with, but what about the M.o.D.? Morton wasn't crazy, yet he and people like him seemed intent on using her invention as a weapon.

Lost in thought, she didn't notice the time till a knock on the door made her jump. She glanced at the clock and frowned. Twenty to twelve. Who on earth would be knocking at this time of night? Martin Sefton, said a little voice in her head. Martin Sefton *and friends*. She got up and tiptoed to a window from which she could see the door.

It was a man, but not Sefton and not, from the look of him, one of Sefton's friends. He was a short, elderly, sad-looking man with glasses and sparse white hair. He was wearing a shabby raincoat and shuffling about in the glare of the security lamp, looking this way and that as though wondering whether to try another knock. Harper let the curtain fall and went to the door which she opened on its chain, peering through the narrow slot.

'Yes?'

'Oh – good evening.' The caller seemed nervous. Apologetic.

'Good evening,' returned Harper, briskly. 'How may I help you?'

The man smiled diffidently. 'I – I'm sorry to be calling at this late hour, Doctor Rye. I wasn't sure you'd still be up.'

'No, well – it's a wonder I am. What can I do for you?'

The man glanced over his shoulder. 'Do you think I might come in for a moment? There are some people by your gate. Young people. They make me nervous.'

'Of course.' She slipped the chain and opened the door. 'Though it *is* very late and I was just going to bed.'

'I know, I'm very sorry.' The man scurried forward and wiped his shoes on the mat.

Harper closed and locked the door and looked at him enquiringly. 'Now, what is it?'

'It's my wife.' There was a catch in his voice as he said this.

'Your wife?'

'Yes.'

'What about your wife, Mr – er—?'

'Lawson. Albert Lawson. She died, you see.'

'I'm sorry, Mr Lawson.'

The man nodded. 'Yes. It's been almost a year now.'

'A year,' echoed Harper. She didn't know what else to say. A horrible presentiment was forming in her mind.

'Almost a year, and I can't get over it. People – friends – keep telling me it'll get better, but it doesn't.' He looked up at the physicist, his eyes brimming with tears. 'I can't live without her, Doctor, that's the truth of the matter. I want her back, and when I read about you in the paper I knew I had to come and see you.'

'Mr Lawson.' He was weeping now, bent over, his face buried in his hands. 'Mr Lawson, I think I know why you've come, and believe me I'd give anything to be able to help you, but I can't.'

'Can't?' Lawson lifted his head. 'Of course you can. If it works with animals, it must work with people. All you have to do is—'

'It's not that simple,' said Harper, as gently as she could. 'Snatching an animal – even an insect

117

– alters history, but in a way that is unlikely to make a significant difference. Snatching a *person* – resurrecting them, in effect – is a different matter entirely. It could have catastrophic consequences. I can't do it, Mr Lawson.'

The man bit his lip, fighting to control his tears. His features shifted, grief giving way to angry scepticism. 'I don't care about history, Doctor Rye,' he croaked. 'All I know is, you have the ability to give me back my wife. You can see the state I'm in. What sort of person would refuse to help a fellow creature in distress, eh – what sort of person?'

'My God!' Harper gazed at him. 'Don't you think there are people *I'd* give anything to have with me again? I had parents, Mr Lawson. Grandparents. A baby who died in her cot. I have the ability to bring *them* back too, but I don't. I haven't. I'm a scientist, Mr Lawson. I have responsibilities.'

'Yes.' The man's voice oozed bitterness. 'You're a scientist all right. A hard, unfeeling scientist, like those who made the atom bomb. You don't care any more about human suffering than *they* did.'

'They cared,' cried Harper. 'They split the atom – they didn't know others would use their work to make a bomb. We can never tell what use our discoveries will be put to, but we have to go on making them – it's our *job*.'

'Don't talk to me,' Lawson shook his head, 'because I don't want to hear anything you've got to say. Open the door and let me out, you heartless monster – I wish I'd never come.'

Harper couldn't watch his departure. She stood aside as he scurried by without so much as a glance at her, then closed the door and slumped against it, weeping.

THIRTY-FIVE

There were five items of mail that Friday morning. Harper brought them to the table and slit the envelopes while Frazer and Kizzy ate cornflakes. One envelope was addressed in green ink.

'Oh-oh,' went Harper.

Kizzy looked at her. 'What's wrong, Mum?'

Harper held up the envelope. 'Green ink. Sign of eccentricity.'

'I didn't know that. Open it – I could do with a good laugh.'

Harper pulled out the letter, smoothed it on the tablecloth and read. Kizzy and Frazer watched her. When she got to the end she chuckled and shook her head. 'Unbelievable.'

'What?' asked Frazer.

'It's from the Friends of Tyrannosaurus Rex.'

'What – the old rock band?'

'No, darling – the even older gigantic lizard.'

'The *dinosaur*?' cried Kizzy.

Harper nodded. 'Listen.' She read aloud.

Dear Doctor Rye,

You don't know me. My name's Danvers Peterson and I'm Secretary of an organization called Friends of Tyrannosaurus Rex. We read about you in the paper and we had an idea. You've got children so you'll know how kids are fascinated by dinosaurs. What if some people got together and built a THEME PARK with REAL dinosaurs in their natural habitat? All we'd need would be a few acres of scrub with perhaps a swampy bit, and you could get the right plants – giant tree-ferns and so on – and the actual dinosaurs. People would flock in their thousands to see it. We'd stand to make a fortune. Of course, we realize we'd have to be careful about security – wouldn't do to have dinosaurs rampaging about the countryside (ha ha!) – but we can cross that bridge when we come to it. My friends and I would pay for the land and see to all the work. What do you think? Looking forward to hearing from you soon.

Yours hopefully.

'Sounds great,' grinned Frazer. 'I can't *wait* to clean up after something that eats a tonne and a half of Kit-E-Kat a day.'

'Trust you to think of something like *that*,' said Kizzy. She looked at her mother. 'Can Rye's Apparatus go back that far, Mum?'

Harper nodded. 'Oh, yes. Theoretically there's no limit, but of course the theme-park idea's ridiculous. In fact,' she smiled, 'there was a film – oh, forty years ago – about this very thing. I saw a clip on TV not so long ago. I wouldn't be surprised if that's where these airheads got the idea from.'

'Will you write and tell this Peterson character it's not on?' asked Frazer.

Harper sighed. 'I don't think so, darling. I've enough to think about without responding to screwball letters in green ink.' She drained her coffee cup and stood up. 'Come on – let's get the two of you to school.'

'Er – hmm,' went Kizzy. 'Talking of letters and school—'.

Her mother looked at her. 'What is it, darling?'

Kizzy told about her interview the previous day with Mr Donovan. 'So you'll get another nutty letter tomorrow,' she concluded. 'Sorry.'

Harper shook her head. 'It seems to me that Mr Donovan picked on you unfairly, though of course you certainly ought not to have said what you said to him. I'll pop in with you this morning and have a quiet word.'

'Oh, terrific,' groaned Kizzy. 'That's all I need. He'll probably hang me in assembly or something.'

'If he does,' grinned Frazer, 'can I have the dosh out of your piggy-bank?'

THIRTY-SIX

Andrew Baggins lived only a couple of kilometres from school, so unless the weather was foul he biked it. It wasn't foul that Friday morning and that was bad luck for Bilbo, because Harvey Parvin was waiting in his Mazda on the one quiet stretch of the boy's route. As Bilbo pedalled towards the car it pulled across the narrow lane, blocking it. Parvin opened his door as the bike wobbled to a stop.

'Morning, Bilbo.'

'Oh – er – morning. Did you want to see me?'

The journalist smiled like a crocodile. 'I will say to

you the word *discretion*, lad. Remember it, do you? We talked about it the last time we met.'

'Yes, I remember.'

'And what did discretion mean, Bilbo?'

'I – er – had to keep quiet about what I told you, and not ask questions, and not go near the Hammer and Anvil till I was eighteen.'

'Correct. So why did you go blabbering to every skunk and his uncle as soon as my back was turned?'

'I – I *didn't*. Honestly. I haven't said a word to anyone.'

'Rubbish, lad! When I left that pub, there was only you and me knew anything about what the Rye woman had been up to, yet a few hours later it was common knowledge. *I* didn't blab, so you must have.'

'But I *didn't*, Mr Parvin. I swear I didn't.'

'Don't give me that, son. I paid for exclusive information and you promptly flogged it elsewhere. You owe me fifty E.'

'But I haven't *got* it, Mr Parvin. I spent it.'

'Ah!' Parvin's expression was grave. 'That puts you in big trouble, my son. *Big* trouble.'

'W-what d'you mean?' Bilbo glanced about him, hoping someone would appear. The journalist closed his door and spoke through the open window. 'Stay there. I'm going to re-park this thing, then you and I must have a little talk. Oh – and don't think about ped-alling off, Bilbo old lad. Kids have been known to get knocked down in country lanes. Happens all the time.'

Bilbo leaned his bike on the hedge as Parvin parked the Mazda. He considered dashing off into the trees, but the man looked fit enough to outrun him and Bilbo decided he'd rather talk to him at the roadside than in the middle of a thicket.

'Right, now.' Parvin rubbed his hands together. 'About this fifty E.'

'I told you, Mr Parvin, I haven't got it. There was this microscope, second hand—'

'I'm not interested in your shopping, son. I want my money. If you don't have it, you'll just have to work it off.'

'Work it off? What d'you mean?'

The journalist shrugged. 'It's perfectly simple. You owe me fifty ecu. You don't have the cash, so you do fifty E's worth of work for me and we're straight.'

'W-what sort of work?'

'Oh – nothing you'd need a university education to do, Bilbo old son. You'd take a few snapshots, that's all.'

'Snapshots?'

'That's right. Got a camera, have you?'

'Yes. A Minolta. What d'you want me to photo-graph?'

126

'Rye's Apparatus.'

'But I – the apparatus must be inside the house, Mr Parvin. I've looked in all the outhouses and it wasn't there. I can't go into that house any more. The Ryes hate me for talking to you. Frazer roughed me up.'

The man shrugged. 'You've stayed there. You know the layout. Find a way in. You've no choice. A debt's a debt, and you wouldn't believe how nasty I can get with little boys who don't pay their debts.'

'All right, I'll try,' mumbled Bilbo miserably. 'When d'you want it done?'

'Sooner the better.'

'And how do I contact you?'

'You don't. I'll be watching. When you've done it, I'll contact you.' He glanced at his watch. 'You'd better be off or you'll be late. Ta-ta for now, Bilbo.'

Bilbo mounted and rode on. He felt as though someone had piled a tonne of scrap iron on his shoulders. Just before the bend, he glanced back. Parvin was standing on the same spot, gazing after him.

THIRTY-SEVEN

'Frazer darling.' Harper looked across the table at her son. 'I want you to do something for me.'

'What is it, Mum?' He was playing with the food on his plate. The square of quiche was the house. He'd surrounded it with a rampart of mashed potato. The peas round the rim of the plate were Martin Sefton and his friends, trying to get in.

'I don't like the idea of leaving this place empty tomorrow. I want you to stay at home while Kizzy and I go into town.'

'Aw, Mu-um!' whinged Frazer. 'We always go

together. I've arranged to meet Ashley and some of the others in the Arndale to look at CDs.'

'I *know* it's inconvenient, dear, but you could phone Ashley, tell him you can't make it.' She smiled. 'It really *would* set my mind at rest.'

'Oh, all right.' He placed a particularly large pea beside the quiche to represent himself. 'At least I'll get a lie-in.'

THIRTY-EIGHT

Bilbo got very little sleep that Friday night. As soon as he lay down in bed the tonne of scrap iron on his shoulders transferred itself to the middle of his chest, making it difficult to breathe. He lay sweating, staring up into a blackness in which phantom lights floated.

He wished he'd never heard of Frazer Rye. He regretted having stayed with the Ryes at Christmas. He wished he'd minded his own business while he was there. Most of all, he wished he hadn't contacted Harvey Parvin.

Fifty E. Can they put you in prison for owing

somebody fifty ecu? Bilbo didn't know, but he knew they could put you there for breaking into somebody's house. Perhaps he should take a chance – refuse to do what Parvin wanted and hope the journalist wouldn't get him jailed. Yeah, that's it! he thought. He felt the scrap iron getting lighter. I won't do it. I just won't. I bet he can't get me for it. He smiled into the darkness as the weight floated away. He rolled on to his side and closed his eyes.

Bilbo was almost asleep when he remembered the film. It was a film he'd watched on telly the week before, about a woman who gambled on horse-races. She couldn't help it. She put all her money on horses – all the housekeeping and everything – and when that was gone she borrowed from a money-lender so that she could keep on gambling. It was a sad film, but the bit Bilbo was remembering was more scary than sad. It was the bit where the woman couldn't pay back the money-lender, and the money-lender got nasty. He didn't call the police and try to get the woman jailed or anything. Instead, he paid two thugs to ambush her one night and break both her legs.

Both her legs. Bilbo rolled on to his back and groaned. I *knew* Harvey Parvin reminded me of someone, he whispered. Now I remember. The money-lender. He looks just like the actor who played the money-lender in the film. What if – what if he doesn't even *try* to get me jailed for his rotten fifty E? What if he gets a couple of big rough guys to wait for me after school and break my legs? Come to think of it, it wouldn't even take two *big* guys – two average guys would do. Or one.

So. He stared at the ceiling. I'm going to have to do it, and I know how, he thought. The window in the guest bedroom has a broken catch and there's a set of ladders in one of the outbuildings. That's how.

And I know when. Saturdays, the Ryes come into Bury St Edmunds. All of 'em. Frazer meets some of the guys. Kizzy has a dancing class. Their mother shops. They have lunch in town, get home around two-thirty, three o'clock. I know all this 'cos Frazer told me. They don't have a dog, thank God, so why not tomorrow? Get it over with.

He groaned as the tonne weight settled once more in the middle of his chest.

THIRTY-NINE

There's nothing like a good lie-in on a Saturday morning after a hard week at school. This week had been particularly hard, what with one thing and another, and Frazer was still luxuriating in a delicious doze at ten o'clock, a full hour and a half after Kizzy and his mother had set off to Bury St Edmunds. He'd probably have kept it going for another hour or so, but in a moment of half-waking he heard an unusual sound.

It was a scraping, rattling noise. It didn't remind him of anything so he told himself it wasn't anything and rolled over, but he couldn't doze off again. A little voice in his head whispered, Hey, aren't you supposed to be on guard? Isn't that why you're here and not in town? He tried pulling the duvet up over his ears but he could still hear the noise, which seemed to be coming from the other side of the house – from the yard perhaps. He was thoroughly awake now, so he sat up and listened.

It *was* coming from the yard. It sounded like something being dragged across the cobbles. Something heavy. He got out of bed and went out on to the landing. As he did so, there came a sound he recognized. It was the solid clunk you get when a ladder is set against a house wall.

Frazer gulped. He hadn't *really* expected anyone to try breaking in while the others were away, but why else would someone put a ladder against the house? No window-cleaner ever came here, and his mother hadn't ordered any work done as far as he knew. Somebody was climbing the ladder now. The sound seemed to be coming from the spare bedroom.

A weapon. He needed a weapon. If he was to repel Martin Sefton, he'd have to be armed. Sefton was a nutcase, like his son. A dangerous nutcase. There was a gun – an ancient sporting gun – on the wall above the fireplace in the living-room. It had been there since before the Ryes moved in and was almost certainly useless, but maybe the sight of it would persuade the climber to retreat.

Frazer scampered down the stairs and into the living-room. He grabbed the gun and bounded back up, panting and cursing. The guy was at the window now – he heard the squeak of it opening. With what he hoped was a blood-curdling yell, he charged into the room, brandishing the gun. Andrew Baggins had one foot on the ladder and the other hooked over the sill. As the demented gunman appeared he tried to withdraw, but his jeans-leg snagged the faulty catch. In trying to jerk it free, the boy flung himself backwards, lost his foothold on the ladder and fell, striking his head on the cobbles. Frazer had recognized the intruder, but his relief turned to horror when he leaned out and saw his schoolmate lying still. He flung the gun on the bed, ran into his mother's room and grabbed the phone.

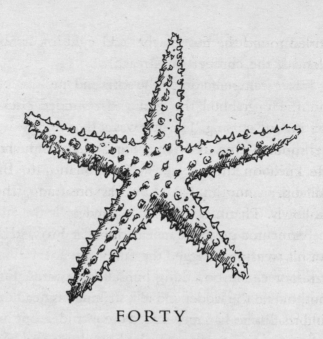

FORTY

'An ambulance is on its way.'

'Th-thanks.' Frazer replaced the receiver and stood for a moment gazing down at it, thinking. What do I do in the meantime? Is this vehicle coming from Bury St Edmunds or Ipswich or Timbuctoo? How long will it take to get here? He wondered if he ought to call the doctor, but that seemed daft when he'd already sent for an ambulance. He ran downstairs and out into the yard, hoping to find Bilbo sitting up, rubbing his head and saying, Where am I? or What happened? or something, but the boy lay motionless, curled round the foot of the ladder with a bubble of blood at the corner of his mouth.

Frazer felt helpless. He wanted to do something, but the only thing he could remember about first aid was that if the patient's air passage was clear, he shouldn't be moved till qualified help arrived. He knelt on the cobbles and put his ear to Bilbo's half-open mouth. The boy was breathing, though shallowly. Thank God for that, anyway.

Frazer got up and tried to look at his watch. He wasn't wearing it, and it was then he realized he was barefoot and in his pyjamas. Remembering the pop fans, he glanced towards the gate, and was relieved to find that nobody seemed to have seen him. He felt he ought not to leave Bilbo, but on the other hand what good was he doing? He hurried indoors, praying the ambulance would come while he was dressing.

It didn't. It had taken him less than five minutes to get his clothes on and drag a comb through his hair and, when he got outside, Bilbo seemed exactly the same. Frazer began to pace, looking from the gateway to his watch to the gateway again. 'Come on,' he whispered, over and over. 'For Pete's sake, come on.' He wished he'd noted the time when he made the nine-nine-nine call, but he hadn't. He wondered what you do if someone stops breathing. He felt sick, scared and utterly useless.

It seemed hours till he heard the siren, though in fact no more than fifteen minutes had elapsed since his call. Thankfully, he watched the two paramedics stretcher Bilbo into their vehicle.

'Is he going to be all right?' he asked.

The man nodded. 'I shouldn't worry, son. Can you contact his next of kin – parents or whatever?'

'Y-yes, I guess so.'

'Good, tell 'em Ipswich General, will you?'

'Ipswich General? Sure.'

He didn't fancy it. What was he supposed to *say*, for Pete's sake? Oh, Mr Baggins, Frazer Rye here. I caught your son breaking into our house. Ran at him with a gun, knocked him clean off his ladder. He fell ten metres on to cobbles and they've carted him off to hospital, unconscious. How's *Mrs* Baggins?

As it turned out, it was Mrs Baggins who answered the phone. Frazer didn't mention any break-in. He told her there'd been an accident involving a ladder, that Bilbo was in hospital and that the paramedic had said there was no need to worry. He was afraid she'd start asking questions, but she didn't. She was obviously puzzled as to why her son had been at the Rye home, but she thanked him for letting her know and rang off.

Probably in the car and off to Ipswich already, thought Frazer. He wished his mother would come home.

FORTY-ONE

The fans of Vulcan Pan were undemonstrative when
the Suzuki returned. Harper, not knowing they'd
seen an ambulance come and go, was agreeably surprised, but the look on Frazer's face as he hurried
out to meet her gave her a jolt.

'What is it, darling – has something happened?'

'You could say that, yes.' Briefly, he related the
morning's events.

When he'd finished Harper said, 'I'll call the hospital, see how he is, then I think I'd better get down
there. You two stay here and I'll call you, OK?'

139

*　　*　　*

It was twilight before the phone rang. Frazer picked up the receiver. 'Mum?'

'Yes, darling, it's me. Is everything all right?'

'Sure. How's Bilbo?'

'He's resting comfortably, as they say. He's concussed and has a broken collar bone, but he'll be fine.'

'Thank goodness for that. Are his folks there?'

Harper chuckled. 'Oh yes, they're here. Baggins senior was quite aggressive when I arrived – red-faced and spluttering, puffed up with indignation – you know the type. His son, injured on our property and all that. We'd be hearing from his solicitor and so forth.' She chuckled again. 'He went ape-shape when I told him his precious son had been breaking in. Refused to believe it, of course, but then Bilbo admitted it and he collapsed like a pricked balloon. Went all subdued. Asked me not to press charges.'

Frazer laughed. 'Bilbo's talking, then? Did he say *why* he was breaking in?'

'Yes. Apparently, he'd sold information to some journalist. A man called Harvey Parvin, who'd paid him fifty ecu and demanded it back when our story hit the front pages. Bilbo'd spent the money so Parvin threatened him – implied that if he didn't get photos of Rye's Apparatus something terrible would happen to him.'

'The rotten swine.'

'I know. Anyway, Bilbo's described the man and his car – number and everything – so I fancy he'll be getting a visit from the police.'

'Good. When're you coming home, Mum? Kizzy's crying for you.'

'I am *not*!' Frazer ducked as his sister's stuffed koala whizzed by his head.

'I'm setting off *now*, darling – you know how I hate hospitals. Put the kettle on, and don't tease your sister – I suspect this Parvin character had a go at her, too.'

FORTY-TWO

'Mr Parvin?'

It was Sunday evening, and the bar lounge of the Hammer and Anvil was busy. Harvey Parvin gazed up at the young man in the grey suit. 'Who wants to know?'

'I'm John Fletcher, Mr Parvin. Constable Fletcher if you prefer. Mind if I sit down?'

Parvin shrugged. 'Please yourself.'

'Thanks.' The constable sat. 'A quiet word, sir, if you don't mind. About a lad called Andrew Baggins.'

'Baggins?' The journalist took a sip of his pint. 'Never heard of him.'

'You sure, sir? Goes by the name of Bilbo, apparently.'

'Naw. Doesn't ring a bell, Constable. Should it?'

'I think so, sir. You spoke to him yesterday. Asked him to take some snapshots for you, to work off a debt.'

'Never.'

'He says you did, Mr Parvin. Says you scared him. He's in hospital because of you.'

'H-hospital?' Parvin slopped beer down his chin. 'Hey, just a minute – I'm not responsible for *anybody* being in hospital.'

'I think you are, sir. The kid was up a ladder, trying to break into the Rye place. He fell. You sent him there.'

'No way!' The journalist shook his head. 'I never told him to break in. That must've been his own idea.'

'So you *did* speak to him, sir?'

'Eh? Oh, all right – yes. I spoke to him. That's not an offence, is it?'

'Threatening behaviour is, Mr Parvin. You threatened the boy, didn't you?'

'I – he broke an agreement. I wanted my money back.'

'So you threatened him. You also threatened a little girl, Kizzy Rye.'

'How—? I never threatened her. I spoke to her, that's all.'

'You told her you might turn into one of those funny men her mum had warned her about. That's dodgy, Mr Parvin. Very dodgy. If I thought you were a man of that sort, I'd have to—'

'I'm not!' Parvin's hand was shaking so much he had to put down his glass. 'Look, Constable. I'm a journalist. All I ever wanted was information – a story. There's a magazine – a French magazine – they'd have paid a small fortune for those snapshots. I never meant to harm those kids – I've got two of my own, for heaven's sake.'

'Then take my advice, Mr Parvin. Go home to them. Leave Long Melford. Leave Suffolk. Go tonight. And if you ever feel tempted to come back, think about this – a woman who can dump a whale in a farmer's field might positively *enjoy* delivering a sabre-tooth tiger to a man who threatened her child.'

Harvey Parvin broke a number of speed records that night as he drove south-west through Ipswich, Colchester and Chelmsford, and it was more than a year before he stopped dreaming about the sabre-tooth tiger under his bed.

144

FORTY-THREE

'So this Parvin character's gone and the media's off our backs,' said Frazer. 'Things are looking up, eh, Mum?' It was Monday evening and Frazer was trying to cheer his mother up.

Harper smiled. 'You're an incurable optimist, darling, and I appreciate your efforts to lift me out of my depression, but I'm afraid it won't work. Parvin's gone, yes, and that's a good thing, but the M.o.D. scared the media away for its own reasons. Morton's pals will descend on us eventually, and God knows what will become of Rye's Apparatus then.'

'I wasn't teased at school today,' put in Kizzy. 'That's another good thing, isn't it?'

Harper smiled again. 'Of course it is, my love. Your mum's nothing but a miserable old sourpuss.'

'It's that man, isn't it?' said Frazer. 'The one who wants his wife back. That's what's *really* got to you.'

Harper nodded. 'Him, and those sad fans out there, and the Friends of Tyrannosaurus Rex, and the M.o.D. Not to mention poor Bilbo in hospital and Mad Martin Sefton.' She sighed. 'So many people, all anxious to use my invention in sick, wrong ways. And I'm afraid they will, in the end. Like Doctor Frankenstein, I've created something only to lose control of it.'

'We can snatch a few more creatures though, can't we?' asked Kizzy. 'Before it all goes wrong?'

Harper shook her head. 'I don't know, Kizzy. It's hard to concentrate when you don't know from one minute to the next what's going to— What's that?'

'Doorbell,' said Frazer. 'I'll go.'

'Be careful, darling – keep the chain on till you know who it is. It's almost dark out there.'

Frazer left the room and returned a moment later with Hazel Ratcliffe.

'Hazel!' Harper rose to greet her friend. 'What a lovely surprise, darling.'

They embraced and Hazel said, 'You sounded so down on the phone I thought I'd better dash over and stop you sticking your head in the disposomat.'

Harper laughed. 'It's not quite *that* bad, my dear. Not quite.'

'So.' Hazel sat down and crossed her legs. 'What's been happening, if anything? I want all the harrowing details.'

Harper and Kizzy brought Hazel up to date while Frazer brewed a pot of tea. The weather was too warm for the laser-blaze, so they sat round an empty hearth and talked as twilight gave way to night. The Ryes were no safer with Hazel there, but they *felt* more secure. She was that sort of person.

'What's been puzzling *me*,' said Harper after a while, 'is exactly what sort of weapon my apparatus might make. I mean – I'm assuming the M.o.D. has a weapon in mind.'

'Oh, that's easy,' said Hazel. 'I spent some time thinking about that, and I think I've got it.'

Harper looked at her. 'Go on.'

'Well.' Hazel took a sip of tea and set her cup and saucer on the small table in front of her. 'What your apparatus does is travel into the past, snatch some creature and transfer it instantly into the present – am I right?'

Harper nodded.

'And you can make this creature appear anywhere you like, yes? In this room, for example?'

'When things go right, yes.'

'OK then – imagine this scene. The leader of a nation at war with Britain has just out got of bed. It is seven a.m. He goes to the bathroom to shave. As he shaves, he is thinking about his day. Breakfast, then the drive to the office for a meeting with his generals. After that, papers to sign, then lunch, etcetera, etcetera, etcetera. You get the picture – an ordinary day in prospect. Suddenly – in the twinkling of an eye, as they say in fairytales – his bathroom vanishes. He's not looking into his shaving mirror any more. He's standing in a strange room a thousand miles away, dripping foam down his pyjamas and staring down the barrel of an automatic rifle. He's a prisoner in England, and it's the day after tomorrow.'

'My God!' Harper gazed at her friend.

'Well, yes – exactly,' said Hazel. 'He'd flip, wouldn't he? It'd blow his mind. And the folks back home would find themselves leaderless.'

'It's horrible,' breathed Kizzy. 'Surely nobody would actually *do* that to anybody?'

'They would, you know,' growled Frazer. 'Some people would do *anything* if it'll help 'em win.'

'I'm afraid Frazer's right,' murmured Harper. 'You've only to look at some of the weapons they *do* use – napalm, for example.' She shivered and looked across at her friend. 'What am I to *do*, Hazel? What on earth am I to do?'

FORTY-FOUR

'Just *look* at the time!' Hazel Ratcliffe started to rise. 'It's ten to eleven, these young people are still up and I have miles to go before I sleep.'

'It's these light evenings,' smiled Harper. 'They're deceptive.'

'Doesn't matter anyway,' said Frazer. 'I *never* have trouble getting up in the morning.'

'Huh!' grunted Kizzy. '*What* time was it when Bilbo woke you on Saturday?'

'That's different, you div — I was having a lie–in.

It's *you* who'll still be snoring at eight o'clock tomor—'

The crash of splintered glass was followed by a heavy thud as a mouldering brick landed on the carpet. The room's four occupants were staring at it when a man's voice shouted through the smashed window. 'We're here, Doctor Rye, just as I promised. Open the door and nobody'll get hurt.'

'It's Sefton,' hissed Frazer. 'I *told* you he was off his nut.'

'The gun!' cried Kizzy. 'Get the gun, Mum.'

Harper shook her head. 'The gun's useless, darling. I want you and Frazer to go upstairs at once. Don't switch on any lights, and stay away from the windows. I'm going to call the police.'

'*I'm* not off upstairs,' protested Frazer. 'There's doors to guard.'

'Well, *I'm* not if he's not,' said Kizzy. '*I'll* have the gun. It put Bilbo in hospital, even if it *is* useless.' She stretched up, lifted the weapon from its hooks and ran to the window.

'Kizzy!' Harper dashed after her as Hazel switched off the light.

'We've got a gun, Mr Sefton!' yelled Kizzy into the night. 'You come anywhere near this house and I'll blow your head off.'

Harper flung her arms round her daughter and dragged her to the floor as a second brick came hurtling out of the darkness and fell, its flight cut short by a heavy curtain.

'Harper, there's something wrong with the phone.' Hazel held the receiver in one hand and jiggled the button with the other. 'I think he's cut the line.'

'I'll try the extension.' Frazer dashed out of the room and up the stairs, but the bedroom extension was dead. 'You're right,' he called. 'The line's been cut.'

From the shadowy garden came a cracked laugh. 'It's been cut all right,' jeered Sefton. 'We're not amateurs, Doctor. You're up against a well-oiled machine here, so you might as well open the door and have done with it. We'll get in anyway, and your kids could be hurt in the process.'

Glass fragments tinkled as Harper got to her feet and peered out.

'You're insane, Sefton,' she cried. 'What d'you think you'd achieve if you *got* inside? You know nothing about my apparatus. You couldn't operate it.'

'No, but *you* could, and you will when we've got a knife at your kid's throat.'

'Never.'

'OK, Doctor – you've had your chance. We're coming in.'

A moment's silence, and then a whistle blew and the garden became filled with moving shadows and running footsteps.

Harper whirled. 'Upstairs!' she cried. 'Quickly. Get into one room and bar the door.'

'What about *you*, Mum?' Frazer had just come down.

Harper shook her head. 'Never mind about me – I must protect the apparatus. Just *go*, please.'

As she spoke there came a splintering crash, and the sound of running footsteps inside the house.

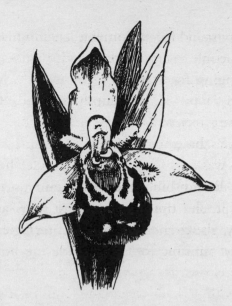

FORTY-FIVE

'Upstairs, the pair of you – go on.' Hazel flapped her hands at Frazer and Kizzy. Harper had disappeared towards her laboratory. There were noises from that direction – shouts and footfalls, and Hazel was anxious to follow her friend. She watched till the youngsters were halfway up the stairs, then hurried down the hallway.

As soon as she'd gone, Frazer said, 'Go on, Kizzy – barricade yourself in your room. I'm off to help.'

Kizzy opened her mouth to protest, but before she could utter a word her brother had vaulted the bannister and dashed off after Hazel.

Kizzy stood for a moment, listening. There seemed to be people everywhere. The house was full of their shouting, yet she couldn't see anybody. Martin Sefton and his friends had obviously broken into the house, but apart from that it was impossible to work out what was happening. Only one thing was certain – Kizzy was *not* about to barricade herself in her room. Brandishing the rusty gun as if she meant to use it, she tiptoed down the stairs and along the hallway, glancing back from time to time to make sure nobody was creeping up on her.

There was a man by the laboratory door. A big man with a bald head and clumpy boots, holding something which looked like a very long rounders bat. Kizzy dodged into a doorway and spied on him but he wasn't doing anything – just standing there.

The lab door was closed. When nobody was shouting or clomping, Kizzy could hear voices. One was Mum's, and there was a man, and another woman – probably Hazel. As Kizzy listened, the man started shouting. She couldn't make out what he was saying but he sounded furious. Mum and Hazel were obviously prisoners in the lab, and the man was probably trying to force Harper to operate the apparatus for him.

Where's Frazer? she wondered. Is he a prisoner too? If so, that just leaves me. What can I *do*? She thought for a moment, chewing her bottom lip. I suppose I could try sneaking out – phone the police. Trouble is, we've no neighbours and the nearest call-box is a couple of kilometres away.

She was still pondering on this when she heard heavy footfalls approaching. She was bound to be seen if she stayed where she was, so she eased open the door she'd been pressed up against, slipped through it, left it open a crack and stood with her eye to the crack. Two men clomped past. One of them said something to the man guarding the lab. Kizzy heard the door open and the same man said, 'We can't find the kid. We've had the place upside down.'

'Looked everywhere,' confirmed his companion.

'No you haven't!' shouted the man who'd been making all the noise. 'You haven't looked where she *is*, or you'd have found her.'

'If anything's happened to my — Ow!' Kizzy winced at the sound of the slap which cut off her mother's voice. It was as much as she could do to stop herself flinging open the door and charging along the hallway with the gun. The man's voice continued.

'Never mind. This dump's kilometres from any-where. She can't do anything. We'll be finished here soon anyway.' There was a moment's silence, then Kizzy jumped as a scream of pain rang out and the man's voice crooned, 'Isn't that right, Doctor Rye?'

Frazer! Kizzy gulped. They're hurting Frazer. Torturing him to make Mum do what they want. I've got to *do* something. Cautiously, she opened the door and peeped out. The bald man was standing by the lab door with the two who'd been searching for her. The door was open and they were looking in, grinning. As Kizzy eased herself into the hallway there was another scream and she heard Harper cry out, 'All right, all right – I'll do it.'

Hitler? Kizzy shuddered. She's going to snatch Hitler. He'll be in this house. In this time. It's sick. It's horrible. Frazer was right – Martin Sefton's crazy. Please let me get out. Don't let them look this way. Oh, please—

FORTY-SIX

She was lucky, or else her prayer was answered. None of the three men glanced in her direction as she sidled along the hallway and into the kitchen. Once there, she was out of sight. She crossed to the door, eased it open and looked out into the yard.

Nobody. OK then – let's get the bike. Quickly she crossed the yard, backed the bike out of the shed and wheeled it along the narrow path which ran down the side of the house. She stood for a moment in shadow, looking across the garden.

All seemed quiet. She'd left the gun in the shed, so speed was her only protection now. She mounted, stood on the pedals and set off diagonally across the lawn, praying that none of Sefton's lot would choose this moment to look through a window.

She'd made it through the gateway, turned right on to the track and was heading for the lane when there came a swishing and a crackling in the bushes and two figures burst out, blocking her way. Kizzy cried out and tried to swerve round them but the manoeuvre was too abrupt. The wheels skidded from under her and the bike crashed to the ground. She lay winded, looking up at the pale blobs of her captors' faces. It was then she saw that they were not Sefton's people, but Vulcan Pan's.

'Let me go,' she panted. 'Please. They've got my mum and brother. They're hurting them. I have to get to a phone.'

'We saw some guys,' said a woman's voice. 'Heard glass smashing. Who are they?'

'Sefton,' gasped Kizzy. 'He's crazy. He thinks Hitler should run the country. He's forcing Mum—'

'Oh my God!' cried the woman. 'I get the picture, kid.' She turned and yelled into the dark. 'Maureen – get over here, quick! Maureen's got a cellphone,' she explained. Hands were lifting Kizzy now – gentle hands that supported her and brushed the dirt from her clothes. 'Who were you calling, love?'

'The police,' said Kizzy. 'Please hurry – if I know Mum, she'll stall those guys as long as she can and that Sefton'll end up killing her.'

FORTY-SEVEN

Frazer lay face down on the bench with his collar in the goon's fist and his arm up his back. At a nod from Sefton, the goon cranked the boy's arm a little higher, causing him to cry out. Harper, at the console, spun round.

'Leave him alone, you great stupid bully – I'm working as fast as I can.'

Sefton smiled coldly. 'You don't look to be busting a gut from where I'm standing, Doctor.'

'It's a complicated procedure, you fool. How d'you

expect me to concentrate when that gorilla's torturing my son?'

The man shrugged. 'The torture, as you call it, will stop when our distinguised guest is standing in this room, and not before.'

Counting on Kizzy and stalling for all she was worth, Harper said, 'Do you speak German, Mr Sefton?'

'What?'

'I said, do you speak German? Your distinguished guest, as you call him, is likely to feel somewhat disorientated when he arrives. He'll need the situation explaining to him, and I'm not at all certain he spoke English.'

'*Speaks*,' rapped Sefton. 'Speaks, not spoke. And no, I don't speak German.'

Harper scoffed. 'And I don't need to ask whether *he* does.' She nodded towards the goon. 'I doubt if he speaks *human*, so how do you propose to greet your hero?'

'*I'll* worry about that,' snarled Sefton. 'You just get him here.'

'Don't, Mum,' gasped Frazer from the bench. 'Let 'em break my arm if they want to – it'll mend.'

'Don't you dare!' spat Hazel, glaring at Sefton from where she was sitting with her hands tied. 'You harm that boy and I'll see you put away for life.'

'Heroics, eh?' Sefton smiled thinly and nodded to the goon. 'Break his arm, Eric.'

'No!' Harper turned. 'I swear if you—'

There was a crash from somewhere in the house, followed at once by a cacophony of screams and yells. Sefton spun round and shouted to the trio in the doorway. 'See what that is. And don't let *anybody* approach this laboratory.'

The men started along the hallway, then stopped. 'What the heck—?'

'What *is* it?' bellowed Sefton. 'What's going on out there?' The screams and yells were deafening.

'It's – it's women,' stammered the sentry. 'A bunch of women, and a kid with a gun.'

'Damnation!' Sefton plunged a hand inside his jacket and pulled out a small automatic. 'Do I have to do *everything* myself around here?' He strode towards the door.

The hallway was jammed with screeching women in T–shirts. They had the three goons surrounded and were kicking and pummelling them as the men spun round and round, seeking space to swing their baseball bats. Between this mêlée and the laboratory door stood Kizzy, pointing her vintage gun at Sefton's chest.

'Drop that!' grated Sefton, levelling the automatic.

'You drop *that*,' shrilled Kizzy. What might have

happened next will never be known, because at that moment the wail of sirens rose above the din, followed by a screeching of brakes as many fast vehicles drew up outside the house. Blue flashes strobed through windows on to walls, floors and faces. Sefton stood a moment as though paralysed, then whirled with an oath and sprinted off along the hallway.

FORTY-EIGHT

The instant the goon realized Sefton wasn't coming back, he abandoned Frazer and fled the room.

Harper ran to her son. 'Darling – are you all right?' she said anxiously. He was sitting on the bench, massaging his arm.

'Bit sore, that's all. What the heck's happening?'

'Dunno exactly. Listen.' She spoke rapidly, watching the door. 'I've come to a decision, and I need a few minutes. I want you to untie Hazel and get her out of here so I can lock myself in. The police have arrived, and I suspect the M.o.D aren't far behind. I need you to block up that hallway for as long as you can. Will you do it?'

Frazer slid off the bench. 'You – you're not going to *hurt* yourself or anything, are you, Mum?'

'No, of course not, silly. Hurry now.'

Hazel's wrists were bound with parcel tape. Frazer ripped it away, pulled the woman to her feet and the two of them left the laboratory. Harper slammed the door behind them. They heard the key turn in the lock. To their left the three goons, now disarmed, staggered about the hallway, trying desperately to dislodge the fans of Vulcan Pan who clung to their limbs and clothing as though to their hero himself, while Kizzy danced round the fringe of the mêlée, cracking the occasional shin with the butt of her gun. As Frazer and Hazel moved to join in, a squad of armed policemen burst through the kitchen doorway. Their leader, an inspector, raised his revolver, fired a shot into the ceiling and yelled, 'M.o.D. police – stand where you are!'

The mêlée became a tableau as the participants turned to find themselves staring down the barrels of half a dozen automatic rifles. Everybody froze except Kizzy, who bent down very slowly, laid her gun on the floor and straightened up, watching the policemen the whole time.

The inspector glanced from face to startled face. 'Which one of you is Doctor Rye?' Frazer looked

166

sidelong at Hazel and pulled a face. Harper had had less than a minute so far.

Hazel nodded imperceptibly and lifted her hand. 'I am.'

The man rapped an order to his squad and strode over. 'Take me to your laboratory, please, Doctor.'

'Certainly,' murmured Hazel. 'This way, Officer.' She turned and led the man past the laboratory door.

Frazer watched till the two of them turned left into a disused former dining-room, then turned and grinned at his sister. 'Nice one, Sis.'

The policemen had separated the goons from the girls and were leading both groups from the house. As Frazer spoke, a constable bent to retrieve the ancient gun. He straightened up, looked at the two youngsters and said, 'Come on – you two as well.'

'But we *live* here,' protested Kizzy. 'Doctor Rye's our mother.'

The man nodded. 'Stay out of the way then, and you'll be all right.'

He was moving away when the inspector reappeared, leading Hazel Ratcliffe by the arm.

'Fitzwilliam.'

'Sir?'

The officer nodded towards the laboratory door. 'Open that.'

The constable tried the door. 'It's locked, sir.'

167

'Then smash it in, man.'

'Yessir.' He lifted Kizzy's gun and began battering at the wood around the lock. Frazer looked at his watch. Four minutes, if that. He hoped it had been long enough.

At the seventh blow the timber gave and the door flew open. Acrid smoke spilled into the hallway.

'Mum!'

Frazer rushed forward but the constable grabbed his arm.

'Wait here. *And* you,' he added, as Kizzy started to move.

'Take 'em outside,' rapped the inspector. 'I'll talk to them later.'

The constable ushered the trio away. The inspector pulled out a handkerchief, held it over his nose and mouth and walked into the laboratory. He didn't know exactly what he'd expected to see, but a bare floor and a smashed console out of which issued smoke and blue sparks certainly wasn't it. His smarting eyes darted about the room and came to rest on the woman.

'Where's the time machine?'

'*Time* machine?' Harper's dirt-streaked face creased into a smile which left a sadness in her eyes. 'What d'you think you're on, Inspector – *Doctor Who*?'

FORTY-NINE

'What did you *do*, Mum?' asked Kizzy, as Hazel's Euro bore them towards Ipswich. The inspector had finished with the Ryes for the moment but his men were still ransacking the house, so Hazel was taking them to stay with her for a few days.

Harper sighed. 'I destroyed it, darling. There was no alternative.'

'In four minutes?' gasped Frazer. 'You smashed it up in four minutes? What about the bits, Mum – won't they be able to reconstruct it from the bits?'

Harper laughed. 'There are no bits, darling. I didn't destroy it in the lab. I'm not *that* daft. I piled all my papers into it and sent the whole caboodle into the past – two thousand years into the past – and to make absolutely sure, I dumped it in the mouth of an active volcano.' She smiled. 'So – those boys back there are searching in vain. There's nothing left but some shorted-out circuitry which might have been used for anything.'

Hazel looked sidelong at her friend. 'You sound remarkably cheerful,' she said, 'for someone who's just scuppered her chance of fame and fortune. Aren't you sad at all?'

Harper nodded. 'Oh yes, dear. I regret the destruction of Rye's Apparatus, but my regret is outweighed by relief – relief that I was able to prevent my invention's use as a weapon. It can never harm anybody now, you see.'

'Mum?' Kizzy's voice sounded odd.

Harper looked at her. 'What is it, darling?'

'Which year did the apparatus end up in?'

Harper shrugged. 'I don't know, dear – not exactly. There wasn't time for pinpoint accuracy, except for dropping the thing into the volcano, of course. Why d'you ask?'

'But you think it was two thousand years ago?'

'Give or take a couple of centuries, yes.'

'Which volcano?'

Harper smiled. 'Guess.'

'I don't want to.'

'Which volcano would *you* have chosen?' pressed Harper. 'Which name comes into your mind whenever you hear the *word* volcano?'

'Vesuvius,' murmured Kizzy.

'Well, there you are then,' she chuckled. 'Vesuvius it was.'

'It's not funny, Mum.'

'Isn't it?' Harper gazed at her daughter. 'You're a strange one, Kizzy – you really are. You behave heroically in the face of all that hassle, and then when it's over you go all solemn on us. What is it?'

Kizzy shook her head. 'It doesn't matter.'

'Yes it *does*,' insisted Harper. 'Tell us.'

Kizzy sighed. 'You say Rye's Apparatus never hurt anybody and never will, right?'

Harper nodded.

'Well – in seventy-nine AD Mount Vesuvius erupted, smothering the towns of Pompeii and Herculaneum and the settlement at Stabia. Thousands died.' Kizzy looked at her mother. 'Seventy-nine AD is two thousands years ago, give or take a couple of centuries. What *made* it erupt, Mum? Could it have erupted because a machine from the future dropped into it?'

'I – I don't believe—' Harper's voice tailed off. Nobody else had anything to say. The Euro sped through the dark.

THE END

Invisible

CHAPTER

1

'D'you want to see something special, Carrie?'

'Like what?' School was over for the day and Carrie wanted to go home. Besides, Rosie Walk was the new girl and Carrie wasn't sure she wanted her for a friend.

'I'm not telling. You've got to come with me if you want to see.'

'Where to?'

'Just the field.'

'There's nothing on the field except goalposts and dandelions and I can see them from here.'

'There's something else, Carrie. Something you wouldn't believe.'

'Oh sure. An alien craft, I bet.' She turned to

leave. Her twin brother Conrad had gone ages ago. Mum liked them to walk home together.

'Better than an alien craft. Tons better.'

'Oh yeah?' She hesitated, curious in spite of herself. She'd heard Rosie was the daughter of travellers and travellers are different. Perhaps she *had* found something on the school playing field that none of the kids had spotted. She sighed. 'OK, where is it?'

Rosie grinned and set off across the grass, which was kept short for games except round the very edge and at the four corners, where dandelions peeped through long blades which trembled in the breeze. Carrie followed, half angry because she'd let Rosie persuade her. *It's probably something really boring, like a hole the boys have dug or a dead bird. I'll slosh her if it's anything like that.*

'Here, see.' Rosie had waded into the triangle of long grass in the farthest corner and was looking down at something. Carrie joined her.

'What?'

'This. D'you see the little toadstools?'

'Sure I see them. Is that it – a bunch of toadstools? I don't call that special.'

'No, but see how they're growing in a ring, Carrie. We call it a fairy ring.'

Carrie scoffed. 'So do we. So does everybody. It's a load of rubbish. I'm off.'

'No, wait a minute. I want to show you what a fairy ring can do.'

'Do? It can't do *anything*, Rosie, except sit there.'

'You're wrong, Carrie. Watch.' Rosie placed a foot on the ring, then brought her other foot behind so that the toe of that shoe touched the heel of the first. Then she lifted the first foot and placed it behind the other, which then rose and repeated the movement. In this way, Rosie walked backwards round the ring, very carefully, arms outstretched for balance. Carrie watched, thinking, *Big deal. She's walking backwards. I can do that* without *a fairy ring.*

She was about to turn away in disgust when something astounding happened. It was so incredible that her mind refused to accept it. She screwed up her eyes, shook her head and looked again. Rosie's jumper and skirt, socks and shoes were exactly where they'd been a second ago, but Rosie was no longer inside them. Where her head should be there was nothing. Her hands were gone too, and her thin brown legs. Her clothes were hanging in mid-air. Carrie screamed.

CHAPTER 2

'Carrie, it's all right.'

It didn't *feel* all right: a school outfit without a wearer, a voice with no mouth. Carrie crammed the knuckles of her right hand in her own mouth to keep from screaming again. *If it comes towards me, I'm off.*

'Don't be scared, Carrie. Keep watching.' The black shoes reversed their direction, walking forward; heel to toe, heel to toe round the ring, as carefully as when Rosie had walked backwards. The grey skirt and maroon jumper moved too, seeming to hover above the shoes and socks. The spectacle exerted a ghastly fascination which kept Carrie rooted to the spot when her every instinct screamed at her to flee. And when the circle was complete there was Rosie, grinning as she let her arms fall to her sides. 'Good, eh?'

Carrie took her hand away from her mouth and wiped it slowly down the side of her skirt. Common sense was already asserting itself, telling her that what she thought she'd witnessed hadn't really happened. *It's a trick of some sort. Has to be.*

'How . . . how did you do that?'

Rosie stepped out of the ring. 'It's the circle, Carrie. The magic circle. Anybody can do it. Any *child*, I mean.' She smiled. 'Grown-ups can't. That's the best part about it.'

Carrie shook her head. 'I don't believe you. What is it, Rosie – hypnotism? Did you hypnotize me?'

'No, of course I didn't. I'm not that clever. It's absolutely true that if you walk backwards round a fairy ring, you become invisible.' She shrugged. 'Doesn't need to be a fairy ring. There are stone circles that'll do instead, like the one above the village.'

'Inchlake Ring?'

'Sure. Kids did it there three thousand years ago.'

'Have *you* done it there?'

'Not yet, but I will. You can too if you want to.'

'I . . . couldn't I try now, in this ring?'

'Sure, but . . .'

'But what?' *I knew it. She tricked me somehow.*

'Well the thing is, you don't become invisible *to yourself*, Carrie. You'll still see your hands and knees and you won't *feel* any different, but you'll be invisible to me.' She shrugged again. 'Means you'll have to take my word that it's worked for you, that's all.'

It's a trick. She has a good laugh while I make a prat of myself, tottering round the fairy ring with my arms out, then tells me I'm invisible. Well OK, if she's that hard up for something to laugh at. There are no witnesses. If she grasses me up to the kids tomorrow, I'll deny it. Who're they going to believe – me, or the new kid? 'All right, I'm ready.'

Rosie nodded. 'Fine. Just step into the ring and do as I did. Be careful. If any part of your foot breaks the circle, it won't work.'

'Right.'

It was harder than she'd expected, walking

180

backwards in a tight circle. A couple of times she nearly overbalanced. And Rosie was right about not feeling anything. She didn't realize she'd completed the circle till the other girl cried out, 'There – you've done it!'

'Have I?' She stopped, looked down at herself and saw what she always saw. *Well – what did you expect? She's having you on, you dork.* 'What do I look like?'

Rosie grinned. 'You don't look like anything, Carrie. There's just your clothes.'

Yeah, I bet. 'What if I step out of the circle now?'

'You'd stay invisible, but I wouldn't if I were you. Not here. Not in daylight. Somebody might come.'

'Right. So you want me to walk forward now, round the ring?'

'Yes. Carefully. Don't want to stay like that, do you?'

You think you're fooling me, but you're not. I'm calling your bluff. 'Rosie?'

'What?'

'Do it again, and this time I'm gonna stand right *there*.' Carrie's sleeve pointed to a spot very close to the ring. 'Let's see you vanish when I can practically *touch* you.'

Rosie nodded. 'Fine. You can shut your eyes if you want, then you can't be hypnotized.' She smiled. 'Walk forward now. Two more steps. there.' They swapped places. Rosie walked backwards. Carrie avoided the traveller's eyes but didn't close her own. She was determined to watch Rosie every inch of the way.

It happened just like before. One second she was there, the next she was not. They hadn't locked eyes so it wasn't hypnotism, and there was no way Rosie could've slipped out of her clothes and hidden in the long grass.

Carrie reached out. 'Give me your hand.' She winced as a hand slipped into hers. An invisible hand. She swallowed. 'Yes, OK. Look, would you . . . ?'

'What?' Rosie chuckled. 'Suspicious character, aren't you?'

'I suppose I am, but it's so *weird*. What I was going to ask was, would you show Con tomorrow? My brother?'

'Sure, if you like.'

'Thanks. I'd better go. Mum goes mad.'

'OK. See you, Carrie.'

'See you, Rosie. If you're not invisible, I mean.'

CHAPTER 3

When Carrie got home her twin was upstairs as usual, playing games on his computer. She knocked on his door. 'Can I come in a minute, Con?'

'What for? I'm busy.'

'I've got something to tell you.' She depressed the handle and pushed the door open.

Conrad swivelled the office chair, scowling. 'I said I was *busy*, Carrie.'

'I can't talk about this in front of Mum and Dad, Con.'

'Why not?' He looked at her. 'What you done – *murdered* somebody?'

'Don't be stupid. It's private, that's all.'

'Aw, all right.' He sighed, killed the sound FX and gave her his full attention.

Carrie told him everything that had happened on the field. When she'd finished he shook his head. 'You're a nut, Carrie. She's having you on. Invisibility's just in stories. It's a scientific impossibility.'

'I *saw* it, Con. She was there, and then she wasn't. Just her uniform, hovering over the ring. And when she reversed the action she re-appeared. I was only two metres away. I saw it happen.'

Conrad snorted. 'Know what *I* think? I think the pair of you have cooked up this tale hoping to make a donkey out of me, but it won't work. You'll have to find somebody else to play your trick on. Somebody less intelligent.' He swivelled his chair, restored the sound and plunged back into his game.

Boys! Carrie considered pulling the plug on the computer, decided against it and left the room, slamming the door.

CHAPTER

4

'You heard Mum, Carrie. *Walk home together*, she said, *not twenty minutes apart like yesterday.* So come on.'

'No. I want you to see what I saw, *then* you can call me a nut.'

Rosie sighed. 'Make your minds up, for goodness' sake. I'm expected home too, you know.'

Carrie glowered at her twin. 'I've made mine up. It's him.'

Rosie studied the boy. 'I reckon he's chicken.'

'I am *not*. 'Course I'm not, but I'm not stupid either. Nobody can be invisible.'

Rosie shrugged. 'Come and prove me a liar, then.'

'You *are* a liar.'

'Prove it.'

Conrad scowled at her. 'All right, but I warn you. When I *have* proved it, I'm going to shove so many fistfuls of grass-clippings down your neck, you'll leave a green trail all the way home.'

The girl nodded. 'Fair enough.'

'Huh!'

'OK.' Rosie had located the ring. 'Who wants to be first?' She looked at Conrad. 'What about you, since you're not chicken?'

Conrad shook his head. 'No way. I told you – I'm not stupid. You'll not catch *me* walking round a fairy ring while you have a giggle with my sister. You go first and I'll watch.' He glared. '*Very* closely.'

'Suit yourself.' Rosie stepped into the circle and walked backwards, slowly, arms outstretched.

Carrie swallowed and glanced at her brother. 'Are you watching?'

''Course I am, you turkey.'

'OK OK. No need to be rude.'

When Rosie vanished, Conrad rubbed his eyes and gaped. There were Rosie's clothes, exactly as his twin had described. Clothes with nobody in them. He looked sidelong at Carrie, who caught his eye.

'Well? Am I a nut or not? If I am, you are.'

He shook his head. 'It's some sort of illusion, Sis. Has to be.' He scanned the long grass with slitted eyes. 'She's hiding. In a hole or something.'

'No I'm not.' A sleeve waved at them. 'See – I'm right here in my jumper.' One shoe left the ground, its sock a tube of grey wool. 'Look. I can balance on one foot.'

'Huh! I still say it's a trick. Let's see you come back.'

'Fine. Watch carefully.' The shoes began to shuffle forward round the circle. The grey skirt kept pace, swinging slightly. Above it drifted the maroon jumper, its empty sleeves stretched out. Conrad strained his eyes to discover some fraud: thin wires perhaps, but there was nothing. The shoes completed the circle and there were Rosie's legs and hands, her reddish hair framing an impudent grin. 'Come on then, Conrad – tell us how it's done.'

'I . . . can't.' He shook his head.

Rosie laughed. 'Wanna see your sister do it?'

He nodded. 'I suppose.'

Carrie took Rosie's place in the ring. Rosie came and stood beside the boy, whose cheeks had turned pale. She looked at him. '*Sure* you're not chicken, Conrad?'

'I'm sure.' He sounded croaky.

'It's just that you're as pasty as a chilled portion, and you clucked just now.'

'Shut your face.'

They watched Carrie vanish, heard her say, 'Have I done it?'

'You've done it,' confirmed the traveller child. 'Hasn't she, Conrad?'

'Y . . . yeah. You can come back, Sis. I believe you.'

'Am I a nut?'

'No you're not. Walk forward, for Pete's sake.' He felt sick.

Carrie reappeared and left the ring. 'Your turn, Con.'

'I know, I know. Give me a chance.' He stepped in. 'Backwards, right?'

The girls nodded.

'And it doesn't hurt or anything?'

'No.'

'And you always come back if you walk

forward? It never fails, I mean?'

'Never.'

'And you'll tell me when . . .?'

'Oh, for heaven's sake get on with it!' This from Carrie.

Conrad did what he'd seen the girls do, and duly vanished. They told him when he'd done it.

'But I can see myself, same as always,' he croaked.

'Rosie *told* you,' snapped Carrie. 'You're not invisible to yourself.'

'Oh, yeah. OK. I'm coming out.'

'Whoa!' Rosie shook her head. 'Not so fast, Conrad. You'll break the circle and stay like that for ever. Can't you just see your mum's face when your uniform walks in?'

'Don't say that!' He slowed down though. Right down. The girls were quite bored by the time he reappeared.

'So.' Rosie grinned. 'What d'you think?'

'It's OK.' Conrad nodded. 'Doesn't hurt or anything, but like . . . what's it good for?'

'Aw come *on*!' Rosie looked at him. 'Think about it. You're invisible. You can go anywhere. Dodge anyone. Get in places free. Listen in to people's conversations. It's terrific fun. I've done it millions of times.'

'Yeah, but . . .' Carrie frowned. 'What about your clothes? They don't become invisible. You'd have to . . .'

'Take 'em off, yes.' Rosie nodded. 'Why not – nobody's going to *see* you. You just don't pick a freezing day, that's all.'

Conrad looked at her. 'You said we'd be able to see each other, though.'

Rosie nodded. 'So what? Have you never seen anybody without clothes?'

''Course I have. It's just . . .'

'You get used to it in no time, believe me.'

Carrie frowned. 'What would we do with our stuff though? I mean, we can't just leave it here, can we? Someone'd find it. Pinch it, probably.'

Rosie shook her head. 'We won't do it here. We'll go up to Inchlake Ring. There's a place we can hide our stuff.'

'How d'you *know* that, Rosie? You only just got here.'

Rosie smiled. 'Inchlake Ring's famous with us travellers, Carrie. We know all the ancient places.'

'Ah. So when do we do it?'

Rosie shrugged. 'Saturday?'

Carrie nodded, smiling. 'Yes, all right. Saturday. What time?'

'Evening's best, when there's less chance of meeting people. Half six?'

'Great. I can't wait.'

Rosie looked at Conrad. 'And you – will you come?'

'I guess.' He looked unhappy.

Rosie grinned. 'We're a gang, then. A gang of three. We should have a name.'

Conrad scowled. 'Why?'

''Cause gangs always have names. How about *The Inchlake Invisibles*?'

'The Inchlake Invisibles.' Carrie tried it on her tongue. 'Yeah, that's cool. The Inchlake Invisibles. Let's call ourselves that, eh, Con?'

'If you like.'

'Well.' Rosie picked up her bag. 'I'm off home. See you tomorrow.' She turned and strolled off, a faint smile on her lips. Her secret was more than just fun. Much more. Yesterday she'd been the new girl, suspect and lonely. Today she was part of a gang. Better still, she was *leader* of the gang. She was going to be all right at Inchlake School.

CHAPTER 5

'Gimme that apple, gipsy.' Lee Kippax stuck out a blunt paw.

Rosie shook her head. 'No. And I'm not a gipsy.'

'My dad says you are. He says you steal and leave muck everywhere.'

'Me?'

'People who live in caravans. Gimme the apple.'

'Get lost.'

'Hand it over, or I'll . . .'

'What's the trouble?' A boy who was passing paused and eyeballed Lee Kippax.

'Shove off, Bunny,' growled the bully. 'It's none of your business.'

The boy looked at Rosie. 'Is he bugging you?'

'He's after my apple.'

'Is he?' The boy tutted, shaking his head. 'Don't you know that's stealing, Kippax?'

'I told you to shove off.'

The boy patted his pocket. '*I*'ve got an apple you're welcome to, Kippax.' He smiled. '*If* you can take it from me.'

'I don't want yours, I want the gipsy's.'

'You're chicken, Kippax. Go peck some corn.'

'I *told* you to . . .'

'Make me.' The boy raised his fists. 'Come on, chicken. Show us how hard you are.'

'Ah!' The bully shook his head and turned away. 'You're not worth it, Bunny. Trust you to stick up for a gipsy.' He glanced at Rosie. 'I'll see you later, kid.' He strolled away.

'What a nasty boy,' murmured Rosie, gazing after him.

The other boy nodded. 'I can't stand him. Made my life a misery when I started here.'

'How?'

'Oh, it was my name. He was forever making fun of my name. Wouldn't leave it alone.'

'Why – what *is* your name?'

The boy smiled sadly. 'You won't believe me if I tell you.'

'Try me.'

'It's Peter Rabbit.'

Rosie giggled. 'It *isn't*.'

'Told you you wouldn't believe me, but it *is*.' He pulled a face. 'Mum's sense of humour. Marries a guy called Rabbit, calls her kid Peter. I'll have my revenge someday.' He looked at Rosie. '*Are* you a gipsy?'

She smiled. 'Not exactly. Mum and Dad are what's called New Age travellers.'

'Ah.' Peter nodded. 'I've heard of them. Whose class are you in?'

'Miss Blackwell's.'

'Hey – me too.'

'Haven't seen you.'

'No, I've been off all week. Flu. You must've started Monday.'

'Yes, I did.'

'Where were you before?'

'Place called Pilgrim. It's near Glastonbury.'

The boy whistled. 'That's a long way off. So you lost all your friends?'

'Yes, but I'm used to that. I've got friends here now.'

'Who?'

'The twins, Carrie and Conrad Waugh.'

'Oh, right. They're OK.' He grinned. 'And now you've got me.'

Rosie nodded. 'Yes. Thanks for rescuing me, Peter. D'you want to join my gang?'

'You have a *gang*?'

'Well, it's just the twins and me at the moment. The Inchlake Invisibles, we call ourselves.'

'Why *Invisibles*?'

Rosie chuckled. 'You'll find out, if you're not doing much tomorrow night.'

Peter was about to pursue the matter when the nine o'clock buzzer went. He shrugged and followed the thin brown girl into school.

CHAPTER 6

Teatime Friday. The phone rang in the Waugh home. Mrs Waugh picked up, listened, then cupped the mouthpiece. 'Carrie!'

'Yes, Mum?' Carrie was upstairs, swapping her uniform for jeans and a T-shirt.

'Telephone. It's Charlotte.'

'Coming.'

'Hi, Charlotte.' Charlotte Webb was Carrie's best friend. They were both ten, but Charlotte was a Catholic and attended a different school.

'Hi, Carrie. Are you doing anything special tomorrow?'

Carrie chuckled. 'Funny you should say that.'

'What d'you mean?'

'Oh . . . nothing. D'you want to meet?'

'I thought we might check out Sizzlers. See who turns up.' Sizzlers was Inchlake's only burger joint. A lot of kids went there Saturdays.

'Fine. I've nothing on till evening.' A stray thought entered her head, making her giggle. *I'll have even less on then.*

'What's funny?'

'Nothing. I'm in a daft mood, that's all. Take no notice.'

'So what time?'

'Oh . . . half ten?'

'Great. I'll see you then.'

'Sure will. 'Bye Charlotte.'

''Bye, Carrie.'

Carrie went upstairs and knocked on Conrad's door. He was on the computer as usual.

'What?'

'Can I come in?'

'I suppose.'

She sat on the bed. 'Charlotte just phoned.'

'So?'

'We're meeting in the morning. Sizzlers. I wondered if I should tell her about . . . you know?'

Her twin shook his head. 'No. It's Rosie's thing, isn't it? She might not be too pleased if we blab to a complete stranger.'

'Charlotte's not a stranger.'

'She is to Rosie, you clown.'

'Yes, but . . .'

Conrad sighed. 'What's the use of asking me, then arguing? Tell her if you want. She won't believe you anyway. She'll think you're out of your tree.'

'I think I will. I might even ask her to meet us up at the Ring.'

'Suit yourself. I might not be there anyway.'

'You've got to come, Con. You promised.'

'No I didn't. The word promise was never spoken. Anyway I'm still thinking about it.'

'If you don't come, I'll never speak to you again.'

Her brother smiled. 'That settles it then . . . I *won't* come.'

'Pig!'

After tea Carrie lay on her own bed, thinking. *It's funny. When Rosie's there, invisibility sounds perfectly reasonable but afterwards – now, for instance – it somehow doesn't seem real. Did it actually happen or was it an illusion, like the Indian rope-trick? After all, thousands of people have watched a man climb the rope – a rope attached to nothing – then vanish into thin air, but we know it doesn't actually happen. It's a shared illusion.*

She thought about it till twilight thickened into darkness and she heard Conrad go down for his bedtime drink, but she reached no conclusion. All she knew was that whatever happened, she'd be at Inchlake Ring this time tomorrow. If invisibility was an illusion it was a good one, well worth seeing again.

CHAPTER 7

It was raining on Saturday morning and Sizzlers was busy. Carrie paused in the doorway, flipped back the hood of her jacket and peered around. Every table was taken. She was about to leave when she noticed somebody waving. It was Charlotte, who must have arrived early and bagged a corner table. Carrie waved back and made her way across, mopping her face with a tissue. Charlotte had spread her stuff on the three vacant seats to discourage others. She cleared one and Carrie sat down. 'Thanks. Rotten morning.' She balled up the sodden tissue and dropped it in the ashtray.

'Yes. I thought we'd check out the park later but it's not fit.'

'Never mind, there's always the mall.'

'True. I want to see if Our Price has the new Split le Beau poster.'

'Oooh, *don't*.' Carrie rolled her eyes. 'You'd think they would have, wouldn't you, seeing he was *born* here?'

'Hmmm. Wish he lived here now, next door to us.'

'Fat chance – about as much chance as winning the lottery.'

'I *know*. Who'd live in Inchlake if they had a choice? Nothing ever happens.'

Carrie giggled. 'Something might.'

'How d'you mean?'

'I'm into something, Charlotte. Something amazing.'

'What sort of something?'

Carrie pulled a face. 'You're going to think I'm crazy when I tell you.'

'No I'm not. Go on.'

'OK, listen.' Carrie told her friend about Rosie, and about what she and Conrad had witnessed on the school playing field on Wednesday and Thursday afternoons. 'So,' she concluded, 'we're meeting up at Inchlake Ring at half six tonight to see what it's like when we take our clothes off and become completely invisible. What d'you think?'

Charlotte toyed with her straw. 'Do you . . . do you believe it, Carrie? D'you think you really did vanish, or did this Rosie character play some sort of trick?'

Carrie shrugged. 'I don't know, Charlotte. I keep telling myself it's impossible, but I *saw* it. I saw Rosie's empty uniform, and Con's. I don't know how anyone could fool me about that.'

'Hmmm. And you're inviting me along?'

'Yes, will you come?'

'I suppose so.' Charlotte chuckled. 'I'm always moaning on about boredom, and this doesn't sound boring, even if it turns out to be nothing but a great big wind-up.'

'It's no wind-up,' said Carrie, tilting her empty can. 'Shall we have another?'

CHAPTER

8

The stones of Inchlake Ring bit into an orange sky as Charlotte and the twins climbed the grassy hill. They'd left their watches at home, but it was probably about six fifteen. Below and behind them, the village lay submerged already in shadow though the sun still shone up here. For two hundred years the footpath they trod had conducted sightseers to the ancient hilltop monument, and for centuries before that, local people had climbed the hill to enjoy the view, to picnic or to be alone with their lovers. This evening though, the children had it all to themselves.

Rosie was there when they reached the top,

sitting with her back against one of the great stones. Peter Rabbit was standing on the so-called altar stone which lay at the centre of the circle, watching the sun go down. Carrie was surprised to find him here.

'I didn't know you were bringing somebody else, Rosie.'

'I didn't know *you* were. Who's this?'

'My friend Charlotte. Charlotte, meet Rosie.'

'Hi, Rosie. Hope you don't mind me coming?'

''Course not.' Rosie looked at Carrie. 'Peter rescued me from Lee Kippax. I owed him one, so I invited him. Do you have a problem with that?'

'No-o.' Carrie pulled a face. 'It's just . . . you know. Getting undressed and that. Feels awkward.'

Rosie stood up, grinning. 'I *told* you – you'll get used to that in no time. Shall we make a start?'

'What do we do?'

'Same as the fairy ring. Stand inside the circle and walk backwards all the way round. It's a lot easier because there's so much room. You're not going to break the circle unless you're a total wuss, and we can all do it at the same time.'

'Do we take our stuff off first?'

Rosie shrugged. 'Makes no odds but I do it after, just in case someone's watching. Come on.'

Rosie and the twins got in line. Charlotte and Peter hung back. Rosie looked at them. 'What's up?'

Peter shook his head. 'You've all seen this done. I haven't. Mind if I watch first?'

Charlotte nodded. 'Same here. I'd like to see you do it before I have a go.'

Rosie nodded. 'Fine. Here we go then.'

Gasps of astonishment rose from the two watchers as the trio completed the circle and vanished.

Charlotte glanced at Peter. 'I see clothes. Just clothes. Do you?'

'Y . . . yeah. I didn't believe, you know?'

'Jesus, Mary and Joseph, nor did *I*. I don't know whether to stand or run away.'

'Don't run.' Rosie's voice, with a laugh in it. 'There's nothing to be scared of. We're still here. We'll take our stuff off now, put it in the hole.'

'What hole?' The voice of Conrad.

'This one over here.' The two children watched as three sets of T-shirts, jeans and trainers walked in line to where a large rectangular recess gaped at the base of a standing stone. Here, the outfits stood in a semicircle and were stripped from invisible bodies, crumpling to shapeless bundles which unseen hands thrust into the recess. Now Charlotte and Peter would have thought themselves alone, if . . .

'Rosie?' This from Peter.

'Still here.'

'Me too.' Carrie's voice.

'And me.' Conrad.

'Come on.' Rosie. 'Your turn. Doesn't hurt a bit.'

Boy and girl looked at each other. 'Shall we?' Peter sounded hoarse.

'I suppose so.' They positioned themselves beside a stone and moved backwards, slowly. Both were afraid, and their fear stretched out time so that it seemed to take forever to go right round. Presently though there came a cheer from the other three, and looking towards the sound they beheld Rosie and the twins wearing exultant grins and absolutely nothing else.

CHAPTER
9

'Have we done it?' Peter held up his hands and examined them. 'Don't look any different.'

Rosie chuckled. 'If you can see the rest of us, you're invisible. Visible people can't see us at all.'

'Yeah, well, I can *see* you all right.' Peter felt his cheeks go hot. 'In fact I don't know where to look.'

Rosie laughed. 'Well there you are, then. You can see us so you're invisible. And if you're *still* not convinced, look at your shadow.'

'Huh?' Away to the west, the sun's rim was touching the horizon. Shadows of standing stones lay long across the grass, but where

Peter's shadow ought to be there was nothing. Rosie giggled at the expression on his face. 'See? The sun's shining through you as if you weren't there. *Now* do you believe?'

'I . . . suppose so, but it's pretty embarrassing. I mean, I don't have a sister. I've never seen . . .'

'Oh come *on*, Pete. I told you – you'll soon get used to it, and we can do anything we like now we're invisible. Follow me, only watch where you put your feet.' She grinned. 'Thistles and broken glass can be disastrous to bare feet.'

She led them downhill. On the bottom stretch of the footpath, just outside the village, they saw an old man walking his Jack Russell terrier.

'Ssssh!' Rosie pressed a finger to her lips. 'No use being invisible unless you're inaudible too. The dog'll come.'

Carrie looked at her. 'Can it see us?'

'No, but it'll know we're here. Dogs go more by scent than sight.'

Sure enough, as the five children drew near the terrier gave a little yip, bounded towards them and began scampering about their feet, jumping up and whining. Its stumpy tail quivered with pleasure as first one child then another bent to ruffle its ears. The old man peered towards the scene of activity, and for an awful moment Carrie felt sure he must see them. It was only when he yelled at the dog that she knew he couldn't. 'Matty! Come 'ere, you barmy mutt – what the heck's up with you?' To him, the animal was fussing round absolutely nothing. The children clamped hands over their mouths to stifle laughter as he came stumping towards them, muttering swear words he'd never dream of using in front of children. The terrier ignored him, and Conrad had to jump back when the man made a lunge, grabbed Matty's collar and clipped on the lead. As he began dragging the dog towards the village the children capered round him, goading the unfortunate Matty into a frenzy of barking and tugging. Where the footpath gave way to a cobbled lane, Rosie made them stop. They weren't quiet enough. Only Matty's barking had prevented the old man from hearing their giggles. They'd need more practice before she'd trust them in the village.

'That was ace,' grinned Conrad as they padded uphill in deep twilight. 'Frantic dog, old guy swearing his head off. I learned four new words.'

Rosie shook her head. 'That was nothing to what we'll do later, but it's really important to keep quiet. If enough people report disembodied voices, scientists'll investigate and then *every* kid will know the secret. It won't be fun any more.'

'Brrr.' Charlotte wrapped her arms round herself. 'It's gone flipping cold since the sun went down. I want my clothes.'

Peter nodded. 'Me too.'

Rosie smiled. 'Race to the top then, OK? Winner hides everyone's stuff. Go!' She went off like a mountain goat and the others followed, too breathless to protest.

CHAPTER
10

Sunday morning, ten o'clock. Rosie opened the rear door of the old ambulance which was her home, descended by way of two metal steps and stood barefoot in the dewy grass, stretching and yawning. It was going to be a beautiful day. Hazy sunshine glowed through a mist which would soon burn off. The lightest of breezes stirred the fluffy heads on the willow herb, freeing seeds which drifted lazily beneath their parachutes, up and away. Down among the stems, spider webs glittered as the sun turned dewdrops to diamonds. Rosie breathed in deeply, her senses filtering the elusive scents of late summer.

'Good afternoon, lazybones.' Her father had carried water from the stream to boil for tea and was watching her through the steam.

She grinned. 'It's only ten o'clock.'

'Only?' He lifted the billy from the Gaz and poured. 'I've been up three hours. There's porridge if you want it.'

'Where's Mum?'

'Gone up the village for baccy.' He smiled. 'I expect she'll get you a choc bar or something, you're so spoilt.'

'I am *not*.' Rosie knelt at the bucket, scooped up icy water and splashed it on her face, scrubbing vigorously with her palms and using fingers to wash inside and behind her ears. 'Spoilt kids have hot water and central heating. I have to make do with this old bucket.'

Her father looked at her, stirring tea with a battered spoon. 'Is that what you want, Rosie? Hot water and central heating?'

She shrugged, reaching for the towel. 'Sometimes, in winter.' She rubbed herself warm and shook her tousled hair. 'No, not really. Not if it means living in one place all the time, in a house.' She draped the towel over a bush, got up and helped herself to porridge.

She'd just started eating when she heard a vehicle approaching. It slowed, pulled off the road and came nosing along the bit of overgrown track their home was parked on. When he saw that it was a police car, Rosie's father got to his feet. Not everybody liked travellers, and sometimes a visit from the police meant trouble.

The car pulled up and two officers got out. One of them nodded to the watchful traveller.

'Morning.'

'Morning.' Rosie's father remained wary. 'Is something wrong?'

'Why, sir, should it be?'

The traveller shook his head. 'Not that I know of.'

'Well that's all right then, isn't it?' One officer, a woman, moved off and started walking round the ambulance as though she might be interested in buying it. The other gazed at its owner. 'I'm Detective Sergeant Springer and that's D.C. Widmead. Can I ask you where you were last night sir, between midnight and four a.m.?'

'I was here, sleeping. Where else would I be?'

'Where else?' The policeman pulled a face. '*Somebody* was over by Inchlake Manor between those hours, sir. I suppose it wasn't you, by any chance?'

'I told you – I was here.'

Rosie looked up at the officer. 'He was, and so was I and so was Mum.'

'Where's your mum now, miss?'

'Gone to the village.'

'I see.' He looked at her father. 'D'you mind telling me your name, sir?'

'Not at all. I'm Daddy Bear, and my wife is Mummy Bear.'

The officer sighed. 'Your *real* name sir, please.'

'That *is* my real name. I chose it myself. It's not against the law, you know.'

'I know the law, sir. I'll call DVLC with your vehicle registration. They'll have your – er – previous name.' He looked at Rosie. 'Baby Bear, is it?'

Rosie shook her head. 'Rosie.'

'Thank God for that.' He glanced towards his colleague, busy kicking one of the ambulance's tyres. 'Mind if we take a look inside the vehicle, sir?'

'What on earth for?'

The officer shrugged. 'You know, sir – routine.' He frowned. 'I could probably get a warrant.'

The traveller shook his head. 'That won't be necessary. Help yourselves. We've nothing to hide, only don't mess the place up. It's our home.'

'Why're they bothering us?' hissed Rosie, when the officers had disappeared inside. Her father shook his head. 'Not sure, sweetheart. Probably investigating a burglary at that place he mentioned – Inchlake Manor.'

'But why *us*, Dad? Why do people assume we're criminals, just because we travel?'

The big man shrugged. 'Who knows? It's an old prejudice. Gipsies. Tinkers. New Age travellers. We're that little bit different, you see.' He chuckled. 'People have a problem with that.'

The officers emerged after a minute or two, empty-handed. The man came over. 'Right, sir, that's all for now. You're not planning to move on in the next day or two, are you?'

The traveller shook his head. 'Not so soon, and when we *do* we're not that hard to find.' He gazed at the officer. 'We've no reason to hide, you see.'

Rosie watched the car reverse down the track and zoom off up the road. Her porridge had gone cold. She scraped it back into the pan and set it on the Gaz, scowling. She hated warmed-up porridge.

CHAPTER
11

One of the best things about Sizzlers was that it was open on Sundays. A juicy burger with all the trimmings makes a fine Sunday lunch, especially if you've only had warmed-up porridge for breakfast. The Invisibles had arranged to meet at Sizzlers at two, but Rosie got there early so she could eat before the others arrived. They'd only get Cokes, having eaten lunch at home, and she didn't want them drooling over her Big Boy two-decker cheeseburger with fries, or her three flavours ice cream in a tall glass with hot fudge sauce and chocolate buttons.

She'd finished eating and the waitress had

cleared when the twins showed up. They joined her and ordered drinks, and by the time the Cokes came Charlotte and Peter were there too. Peter slid into a red plastic seat and grinned. 'You know what we should do, don't you?'

Carrie looked at him. 'What should we do, Pete?'

'We should order five of everything on the menu, scoff the lot, then go in the toilets and make ourselves invisible so we could sneak out the door without paying.'

'We'd need a ring, dummy. And what about our clothes?'

'We chuck 'em out the window, pick 'em up round the back. Easy-peasy.'

Carrie laughed. 'You're a criminal deep down, aren't you, Pete?'

Peter shook his head. 'No, not really. I was joking.'

Rosie nodded. 'I hope so, Peter. You see, there's a rule about that.'

'What d'you mean? *Whose* rule?'

'My rule. It says we never use our invisibility to do bad things, like stealing.'

Conrad looked at her. 'You mentioned getting in places free. That's the same as stealing.'

Rosie sighed. 'I didn't mean we'd actually *do* it, Conrad. I was giving examples of what's possible, that's all.'

'Oh, right.' He smiled. 'And are there any other rules, Rosie, while we're at it?'

She shook her head. 'No, just the one.'

'What if one of us breaks the rule?'

Rosie shrugged. 'Anyone who breaks the rule is out of the gang.'

'But he can still make himself invisible.'

'Yes, but you'd be surprised how little fun it is by yourself. Anyway,' she smiled, 'none of us is going to break the rule, so it doesn't matter.' Her smile faded as she continued, 'There *are* crooks about, though. Visible ones. We had a visit from the police this morning.' Briefly, she told them what had happened at breakfast-time.

When she'd finished, Charlotte nodded. 'My dad heard about it in the paper shop. They used a glass-cutter and got away with two priceless paintings.'

Conrad arched his brow. 'Priceless?'

'Well – they're worth millions. Dad says it's happening all over. A gang of art thieves, breaking into big houses, taking pictures and statues and stuff. The cops reckon it goes to crooked collectors abroad.'

'Wow! And I thought nothing ever happened in Inchlake.'

Charlotte shook her head. 'It's not just Inchlake, Con. It's the whole area.'

'Yeah, but like . . . the gang's *headquarters* might be here, mightn't it? Hey, listen.' His eyes shone with excitement. 'We could investigate, right? *The Inchlake Invisible Detective Agency*. What d'you reckon?'

Carrie gazed at her twin. 'What do I reckon? I reckon you're barmy, Con. A total nut.' She appealed to the others. 'Am I right?'

Rosie pulled a face. 'I dunno, Carrie. Maybe, but I'll tell you what – we *could* go invisible and take a look round Inchlake Manor. Search for clues. It's something to do on a boring Sunday, isn't it?'

Peter frowned. 'There's a problem.'

Rosie looked at him. 'What?'

'Clothes. Where to take 'em off and where to hide 'em. It's Sunday afternoon and the sun's shining. That means flocks of people up at Inchlake Ring.'

'No prob.' This from Conrad.

His sister glanced at him. 'What d'you mean, no prob?'

'We're talking about the Manor, right? Well, there's an old building in the grounds. The ice house, they call it. Nobody ever goes there. We could use that.'

Rosie shook her head. 'We need a *ring*, remember.'

'It *is* a ring. The ice house, I mean. It's round. Would that work, Rosie?'

Rosie shrugged. 'One way to find out. Come on.'

CHAPTER
12

They'd expected police activity, but everything seemed quiet as the five children passed between the great granite gateposts of Inchlake Manor. Weeds poked through the gravel of a driveway narrowed by long-neglected rhododendrons crowding in on either side. At this time of year the house lay hidden beyond a dense screen of foliage. Provided no vehicle followed them through the gateway there was little chance of their being seen.

Rosie looked at Conrad. 'Where's this whatsit then – ice house?'

'See that?' The boy nodded towards a gap in the rhododendrons. 'Through there. There's a pathway curves right round the back of the house.'

'How d'you know, Con? Ancestral home, is it?'

He shook his head. 'A bunch of us used to mess around here, exploring.'

'Ah.'

It was dark under the trees. The path was narrow, slimy and overgrown. It made Carrie think of frogs and toads, though she didn't see any. Her twin went first, leading them in a great curve till a weird structure appeared in the tangle to their right. It was shaped like an igloo but was much bigger, built with great blocks of stone. Conrad held up a hand and they stopped.

Rosie gazed at the ice house. 'Where's the door?'

'Halfway round. Careful when you go in – floor's below ground level.' He led the way round the igloo's mossy curve to a doorless entrance where he sat down, dangling his legs into darkness.

Charlotte peered over his shoulder. 'Ugh!' She shuddered. 'It's pitch-black and it stinks. I'm not going in there.'

Conrad chuckled. 'It only smells like mush-rooms, and it's not really dark once your eyes get used to it. Here goes.' He planted his palms on the rim and lowered himself, feeling for the floor with his trainers. When he dropped and turned, his chin was level with the ground.

One by one the others followed. Conrad helped them down. They stood in the light from the door-way and peered nervously into the blackness. Peter thought of monsters. Charlotte fancied she could see something moving. Conrad let out a sudden whoop whose echo was augmented by the screams and gasps of his companions.

'Daft beggar!' snarled his twin, when she'd recovered enough to speak. 'Scared me half to death.'

'And me the other half.' Peter's voice sounded hoarse.

Conrad was laughing so much he had to lean on the wall to keep from collapsing.

Very funny, Rosie thought but didn't say. *But not half as funny as what I'll do to you when you least expect it.* Aloud she said, 'Did we come here to play silly games, or do we go invisible and get on with our investigation?'

'Investigation,' voted Carrie. '*If* this place works like a stone circle.'

Rosie nodded. 'It'll work. I'll go first if you like.'

'Go on then, but I vote we keep a hand on each other's shoulders all the way round so we don't get separated. Will it be OK like that?'

'Don't see why not. Everybody set? Then let's go.'

CHAPTER 13

It worked, as Rosie had hoped it would.

They left their things on a dank ledge and scrambled out of the ice house. It felt good to breathe fresh air, though it was a bit cold. They moved slowly between the trees, careful where they put their feet. Presently the foliage thinned and there loomed the Manor, looking semi-derelict with its faded paintwork and dusty windows.

Rosie pulled a face. 'Bit of a dump, isn't it? Inchlake Manor. I expected something really posh.'

'Yeah, well.' Conrad nodded. 'It used to be posh when the family had it, but there's only the old lady left now. Miss Massingberd. She can't keep up with it.'

'Hmm.' Rosie shook her head. 'Can't imagine priceless paintings here, can you?' She frowned. 'Wonder how the thieves knew?'

They worked their way round to the front of the house, keeping to the fringe of the trees. A flight of mossy-looking steps led up to great double doors, which were closed. Somebody had parked a yellow Polo at the foot of the steps.

'Who's is that, d'you reckon?' whispered Charlotte. 'Doesn't look like a police car.'

Conrad shrugged. 'Search me.'

His twin giggled. 'That wouldn't take much doing right now, Con.'

'Shut up.'

'Let's take a closer look.' Rosie set off across the lawn. The others hung back and she turned, grinning. 'It's OK. You're invisible, remember?' They'd forgotten, which was easy when they could see each other. They followed, wearing sheepish expressions.

There was a sticker on the inside of the car's windscreen. NURSE ON CALL.

Rosie nodded. 'That explains it. District nurse. Miss Massingberd must be pretty decrepit.'

'She is,' confirmed Conrad. He looked at Rosie. 'What we gonna do?'

'Find a way in, have a snoop round.'

'You mean inside the house?'

'Sure, why not? Nobody's going to see us.'

'So we just march through the door?'

'Well, perhaps not *this* door. No point taking unnecessary risks. There'll be a side door somewhere. Stay close, and no talking.'

They crept along the front of the Manor, peering into windows. Great dim rooms lay beyond the streaky panes, their furniture shrouded in sheets. Turning a corner they found a conservatory built onto the south wall of the house and, in the angle of the wall and its cast-iron frame, a door which squealed open when Rosie tried it. Hardly daring to breathe, the Inchlake Invisibles tiptoed inside and stood on a floor of terracotta tiles, gazing around.

It seemed Miss Massingberd used the conservatory as a sun lounge. A small table stood beside a wicker armchair. There were books and tea things on the table, crumpled cushions in the chair and a footstool nearby. It looked as though the old lady might have been sitting here until a few minutes ago. Behind the furniture an open door gave on to a dim corridor. Many of the conservatory's windows had cracks in them, and Rosie noticed that one had no glass at all but was boarded up with a sheet of plywood. The wood looked new, and Rosie wondered whether this was where the thieves had got in. She was walking towards it when Carrie hissed a warning. A door in the corridor had opened and a frail old lady was shuffling towards the conservatory, one hand hooked through the arm of a strapping nurse.

CHAPTER
14

'Freeze!' hissed Rosie. 'Not a word.'

It felt weird, standing like statues as the two women came slowly across the tiles. Impossible to believe they wouldn't be seen the instant Miss Massingberd glanced up. Or the nurse. Carrie began rehearsing an excuse. *The door was open. We were exploring. We thought it was an empty house . . .*

The nurse steered Miss Massingberd to her chair, practically brushing against Charlotte, and steadied the old lady as she sank into it. 'There.' Charlotte had to take a rapid step backwards as the nurse straightened up. 'Are you *sure* there isn't somebody who would come and sit with you? It must be a nasty shock, knowing thieves have been in your house.'

Miss Massingberd shook her head. 'Not so much a shock as a disappointment, dear.'

'Disappointment?'

'Oh, yes. You see, I had planned to sell those paintings to pay for repairs to this place. It's falling to pieces, year by year. A hundred jobs need doing and there's no money.'

The nurse looked sympathetic. 'Yes, it must take a lot of keeping up, a place like this. Weren't the paintings insured?'

'Oh no, dear. Far too expensive, insurance. They expect you to install all sorts of alarms and lights and whatnot which cost a fortune, and when you say you can't afford it they refuse to insure.'

The nurse shook her head. 'I'm sorry, Miss Massingberd, really I am.' She smiled. 'If you're sure there's nothing more I can do for you, I'd best be on my way.'

'Windows.'

'Windows?'

'Yes, windows. Or rather, their *frames*. They're the most urgent problem. Rotten wood, you see.'

'Ah – yes, I see. Well . . .'

'Practically falling out, some of them. Rattle on windy nights. One good storm and – whoosh! – they'll be gone. Then where shall we be?'

'I . . . really don't know, Miss Massingberd. I'll see you tomorr . . .'

'Man was up just a couple of days ago. Carpenter fellow from the village, what's his name? Kipper. Kepler. Something like that. I'd called him to come and inspect the frames, you see. Prepare an estimate. Well, I expected there'd be money, from the paintings. Now . . .' The old lady shrugged. 'Nothing. Not a bean. Better if I'd sold the bally pictures years . . .' She broke off and gazed at the nurse. 'Don't you have patients waiting, dear? Oughtn't you to be on your round, or whatever it's called?'

Charlotte let out a long, careful sigh as the nurse picked up her bag and departed in an antiseptic waft. *Thought she'd never go.* She looked across at Rosie, who nodded towards the door and mouthed the word *out*. Miss Massingberd's head was nodding. With visits from the police and the nurse she'd had a tiring morning, but if she'd known five invisible callers were tiptoeing past her chair, she'd have found it less easy to fall asleep.

CHAPTER
15

The five had put twenty metres between themselves and the conservatory when Carrie whistled.

'Jeez, that was scary! You don't *feel* invisible, do you?'

Peter shook his head. 'No, but you certainly feel *bare*.' He giggled. 'I kept expecting the old bird to look at me and say, *Where are your* clothes, *young man*?'

Conrad nodded. 'Me too. I couldn't believe we could just stand there and they wouldn't know.'

'What about *me*?' squealed Charlotte. 'That nurse actually brushed me with her skirt as she went past. I nearly died.'

Rosie smiled. 'You all did fine. Much quieter than last time.'

Peter scoffed. 'We flipping well *had* to be didn't we, with people two metres away.'

'Millimetres,' amended Charlotte.

Rosie nodded. 'That's another thing. You've got to make sure nobody actually *touches* you, because that's an even bigger give-away than hearing something.'

Conrad looked back at the Manor. 'Are we leaving already? We didn't do much searching for clues.'

Rosie shook her head. 'We don't *have* to leave. I thought you might have had enough, what with the scare and all. Who's for staying?'

'I'm all right,' murmured Peter.

'Me too.' This from Charlotte.

Carrie nodded. 'We're OK, Rosie. What shall we . . .' She broke off at the sudden noise of a car engine.

Rosie grinned. 'Don't panic, it's only Florence Nightingale.'

'Who?'

'The nurse, you spack. Leaving.'

'Oh. Oh yeah.'

They stood on the overgrown lawn, listening.

The engine noise receded till the wind in the grass was louder. Then they wandered back towards the house, giving the conservatory and its sleeping occupant a wide berth.

They circled the Manor, combing neglected flower-beds and peering into shrubs, finding nothing. When they reached the south wall again, Rosie advanced alone to examine the freshly boarded window and the ground under it. Through the streaky panes she could see the back of Miss Massingberd's chair and the top of the old lady's head. Traces of a silvery powder on the window frame meant the police had dusted for fingerprints. There was nothing else.

'Waste of time,' growled Peter as the five picked their way towards the ice house.

Rosie shrugged. 'Good invisibility practice, if nothing else.'

'Hope nobody's swiped our stuff,' murmured Charlotte.

'Hey.' Carrie's eyes sparkled. 'What if the thieves have hidden the paintings in the ice house?'

Her twin scowled. 'Why the heck would they do *that*, dipstick?'

'I dunno. Too heavy to carry, perhaps.

You know – come back later with a truck?'

Rosie grinned. 'Suppose they come back while we're in there, just as we go visible?'

'Oooh!' Charlotte shivered. 'Don't say that, Rosie, for goodness' sake. It's going to take me all my time to go back into that place as it is.'

The ice house lay silent under its canopy of trees. Their clothes were undisturbed. They dressed quickly, crowded into the half-light by the door. Truth was, they'd spooked themselves with talk of the thieves. They knew they had to circle once more in the inky blackness and nobody fancied it.

Halfway round, a heavy hand fell on Conrad's shoulder and a voice growled in his ear, *Gotcha, you miserable young snooper.* The boy's scream nearly blew the roof off, and it was ten minutes before he was able to complete the circle on rubber legs. Rosie had got her revenge.

CHAPTER 16

Mummy Bear plucked the pegs from a pair of jeans, folded the garment over her arm and handed the pegs to Rosie, who dropped them in the bag. A sunny day and a light breeze had dried the washing beautifully. Now, at dusk, big moths looped round the fire Daddy Bear was tending a few metres away. He'd built it downwind of the line so smoke wouldn't spoil the clean clothes. He'd cook dinner over the fire and later they'd sit round it till bedtime, talking.

'So.' Mummy Bear took down a jumper. 'What did you do today, Rosie?'

'Oh, I met some of the kids at Sizzlers.' Rosie

dropped pegs in the bag. 'We went invisible and had a snoop round Inchlake Manor.'

'You did? What for?'

'I thought we might find a clue to who burgled the place.'

'And did you?'

'I'm not sure.'

'Ah-ha.' The line was empty. Her mother dumped the last of the clothes in the basket and straightened up. 'You *are* being careful who you teach invisibility to, aren't you, sweetheart? It's a dangerous skill in the wrong hands, you know.'

Rosie nodded. 'I know, Mummy Bear. I wouldn't give it to anybody who'd use it in bad ways.'

Mummy Bear smiled. 'I know you wouldn't, Rosie. Come over to the fire and tell Daddy Bear and me all about these friends.'

'Well, there are four of them,' began Rosie, when they'd settled themselves. Daddy Bear leaned forward with a long spoon to stir the stewpot. 'Two girls and two boys. The girls' names are Carrie and Charlotte, and the boys are called Peter and Conrad. Carrie and Conrad are twins. Charlotte goes to a different school but she's Carrie's best friend. Peter saved me from a bully.'

Daddy Bear smiled through fragrant steam. 'It's good you have friends, Rosie. I bet I can guess what you're calling yourselves.'

'What?'

'The Inchlake Invisibles.'

'How'd you *know* that?'

He laughed. 'It's not that hard, sweetheart. Let's see: so far this year we've had the Pilgrim Invisibles, the Appleby Invisibles and now the Inchlake Invisibles. Last year it was the Whitby Invisibles and the Kirk Yetholm Invisibles. Next year . . .'

'Yeah, OK OK.' Rosie lifted a hand. 'I know I'm not big on originality, but what *can* you call a gang that makes itself invisible?'

Her father chuckled, shaking his head. 'It doesn't matter, honeybunch. You make friends everywhere we drag you, and *that*'s what matters. Bring 'em over one evening and we'll have a barbecue.'

Rosie grinned. 'Thanks, Daddy Bear, that'll be really cool.'

Daddy Bear smiled. 'Better do it before the end of the month or it won't be just cool, it'll be bitterly cold.' He lifted the spoon and tasted the stew. 'Mmmm. I reckon this is just about ready if you want to pass your plates.'

CHAPTER
17

'Rosemary Walk.' Miss Blackburn plucked Rosie's essay from the top of the pile and frowned at it. 'I asked everybody to write a piece entitled *My Family*. I expected *factual* pieces.' She looked at Rosie over the top of her half-moon glasses. 'You may remember we talked last week about different *sorts* of writing. Fiction was one sort. What *is* fiction, Rosemary?'

'Miss, it's made-up stories with characters instead of real people.'

'And factual writing?'

'Miss, factual writing's about real people and actual events, like history and that.'

'Correct. So why did you give me a piece

240

which mixes fact with fiction?'

'I didn't, miss. Everything's true that I wrote.'

'No, Rosemary, it is not.' The teacher read from the top sheet. 'I have no sisters or brothers. There's just Mum and Dad and me. My dad's name is Daddy Bear, my mum's is Mummy Bear.'

Some of the children sniggered. Miss Blackburn gazed at Rosie. 'Daddy Bear is not a name, you silly girl, and neither is Mummy Bear. Since your surname is Walk, I assume your parents are Mr and Mrs Walk. If you don't know their first names, Mr and Mrs Walk will be quite sufficient.' She skated the essay across Rosie's table. 'Corrections in the margin, please, and no more fairy tales unless I ask for them.'

As the teacher moved on, Rosie straightened the essay and rested her fists on it, blushing furiously.

Carrie leaned towards her. 'Never mind, Rosie. She'd have a cow if she knew what we call *her*.'

Rosie smiled briefly. Miss Blackburn's nickname was *Blackbum*. 'I know, Carrie, but these *are* Mum and Dad's names. Dad says you've got the right to be called anything you choose.'

'Ah, but your dad's not in old Blackbum's class, is he?'

'Wish he was. He'd sort *her* out, quick-sticks. Anyway, can you come to a barbecue Friday after school?'

'A barbecue? Where?'

'Our place. And will you ask Charlotte?'

'I'll have to ask my mum first. She's not keen on me going in the woods in broad daylight, never mind after school. Can Conrad come, if we get permission?'

'"Course. All the Inchlake Invisibles. Tell your mum you'll be perfectly safe with my folks. I'll mention it to Peter at break.'

'Are you *chattering*, Rosemary Walk?' Miss Blackburn's voice was like a whiplash. The two girls sprang apart.

'Just borrowing Carrie's ruler, miss.'

'Hmmm.' The teacher eyeballed Rosie. 'You will be sure and give it *back*, won't you, Rosemary? Can't have things going astray in our classroom, can we?'

'No, miss.'

CHAPTER 18

'I'm really sorry, Rosie. I can't believe old Blackbum *said* that.'

'It's OK, Carrie. Not your fault. Some people are like that about travellers.' It was break-time. The two girls were in a far corner of the playing field, close to the fairy ring.

Carrie shook her head. 'Not fair though. You'd think a teacher'd know better.'

Rosie pulled a face. 'She's my gran's age, and my gran used to say this nursery rhyme to me when I was little:

> *My mother said*
> *I never should*

Play with the gipsies
In the wood.

'They used to tell kids gipsies would steal them, you see. Take them away. No wonder older people think gipsies are thieves.' She grinned. 'I bet Gran would've had a fit if she'd known her own daughter was about to become a traveller.'

'Get your ruler back, did you?' The girls turned to find Lee Kippax leering at them. He was with Carl Foxcroft and Rex Fairclough as usual.

Carrie looked at him. 'Yes I did, not that it's any of your business.'

The bully nodded. 'And is your dad going to give the pictures back too, gipsy?'

'My dad hasn't got any pictures, apple-thief.'

'Oy!' Kippax raised his fist. 'Don't call *me* a thief. Nobody calls Lee Kippax a thief.'

'Don't call me gipsy, then. The correct term is *traveller*.'

'Ho.' He put on a la-di-da voice. 'So that's the *correct* term, his hit? Haim sorry hif I caused hoffence.' His two friends guffawed.

'Go away, Kippax.' This from Carrie. 'And take your mutants with you.'

'That's not very nice, is it?' He looked at his companions. 'D'you hear what she *called* you, lads? Mutants. I'd be hurt if it was me. You know – inside. I'd want to lash out. Fancy lashing out do you, Carl? Rex?'

A slow smile warped Foxcroft's features. 'Yeah. Now you come to mention it, Kipper, I *do*. How about you, Fairy?'

Fairclough nodded. 'I like a good lash out, Foxy, you know that.'

'So what are we waiting for?' Kippax advanced on the two girls. This corner was a long way from the staffroom window. There'd be no witnesses.

'Wait.' Rosie held up a hand. 'Watch.' She stepped into the ring and shuffled backwards, arms outstretched.

The bully hesitated. 'What's your game, gipsy? How d'you mean, *wait*? Nobody tells Lee Kipp . . . huh?' He shook his head, rubbed his eyes and goggled at Rosie's empty uniform. '*Carl? Rex?* Has she just . . . am I going nuts?'

'She's vanished,' croaked Foxcroft. 'That right, Fairy?'

'Y . . . yeah.' Fairclough scowled at Carrie. 'Here – how's she *do* that, kid?'

'Never mind how I do it.' Rosie's voice came from the air above her empty clothes. 'Think about *this* – I can vanish, and I can do other things too – stuff you wouldn't believe. So if I were you I'd think twice before messing with me, or any of my friends. OK?'

'Er . . . yeah, right. Come on Kipper, let's . . .'

The trio drifted away with many backward glances. Rosie waited till they were off the field, then went visible. She grinned at Carrie.

'Useful skill, or what?'

CHAPTER
19

Halfway through Maths Miss Blackburn said, 'Are you feeling ill, Lee Kippax?'

Lee was sitting with his elbows on the table and his face in his hands. He shook his head. 'I dunno, miss.'

'You don't know whether you feel ill or not?'

'No, miss.'

'Is it the *work*? Something you don't understand, perhaps?'

'No, miss, it's not the work.'

'Well, if you're not ill and you understand the work, why aren't you getting on with it?'

'Dunno, miss.'

'No, Lee, and neither do I. If you have no

explanation for *me*, perhaps you'd care to explain yourself to Mr Beecroft. Would you?'

'If you like, miss.'

'It's not a question of what I *like*, Lee. You're here to work, and if you won't work you must expect to suffer the consequences. Go to Mr Beecroft's office at once and tell him why I sent you.'

'Come.' The Head looked up as Lee walked in. 'Now, Lee Kippax, what can I do for you?'

'Sir, Miss Blackburn sent me because I wasn't getting on with my work.'

'Really?' He gazed at the boy under beetling brows. 'And *why* weren't you working, Lee?'

'Dunno, sir.'

'Something the matter at home, perhaps? Something you'd like to talk to me about?'

'No sir. Well . . . yes, sir, but it's not about home. It's about that new girl – Rosie Walk.'

'A girl.' The brows arched. 'Not in *love* are we, Lee?'

Kippax blushed furiously. 'No, sir. She . . . can make herself disappear.'

'*Disappear?*' The Head's eyes narrowed. 'What on earth are you talking about, boy?'

'Please, sir, I *saw* her. On the field. Carl Foxcroft and Rex Fairclough saw her too.'

Mr Beecroft shook his head. 'Never mind Carl Foxcroft and Rex Fairclough. We're talking about *you*, Lee Kippax.' He clasped his hands on the desktop, sat back in his swivel chair and sighed. 'Go on.'

'Well, sir, me and . . . we were on the field, and the new girl was there with Carrie Waugh.'

'And?'

'We . . . I said something to them, sir. Sort of a joke, and then the new girl got in the fairy ring and the next thing I knew . . .'

'*Fairy ring?*'

'Yessir, there's a fairy ring. She got in it and like – vanished. There was just her clothes, sir.'

'Just her clothes? You mean, in a heap on the ground?'

'No, sir, they were standing up, but she wasn't inside them. They were like *hollow*, sir.'

'I see.' The Head leaned forward, scrutinizing Lee's features. 'Have you been *sniffing* something, laddie?'

'No, sir.'

'Have you *swallowed* something, then? A pill, perhaps? Did you take a pill from somebody?'

'No, sir, it was real, honest. We all saw it.'

'Hmmm.' Mr Beecroft sat back and folded his hands on his stomach. 'You realize that what you've told me is quite impossible, don't you?'

'I . . . *thought* so, sir, yes, but . . .'

'And yet you're convinced you saw it?'

'Yessir.'

'Well, I can't pretend I understand, Lee, so I think perhaps we'd better have your father in.'

'No, sir, don't tell my dad, please. He'll *kill* me.'

'Oh *come* now, Lee, why should your father *kill* you just because you've suffered some sort of hallucination? He might want to take you to a *doctor*, but . . .'

'I made it up, sir.'

'Ah, now that's more like it, Lee. *That* I understand perfectly.' He leaned forward. 'Feeling lazy, are we? Bit bored, so we decide we'll invent a story to liven things up a bit. Is that it?'

The boy nodded miserably. 'Yes, sir.'

'Yes, and perhaps we can get the new girl into trouble while we're about it, eh? Little bonus, so to speak?'

'Yes, sir.'

'That's what I thought.' He sat back and

regarded Lee through half-closed eyes. 'Like most bullies, Lee Kippax, you're a fool. What are you?'

'A fool, sir.'

'A fool who doesn't fool anybody, and that's a sad and sorry sight. What is it?'

'A sad and sorry sight, sir.'

'Absolutely. So you're bored, eh? Looking for a bit of a *challenge*?'

'Yes, sir.'

'All right – here's a challenge for you. Go back to your classroom, apologize to Miss Blackburn, complete the work she set and bring it to me, correct and beautifully presented at three thirty, by which time I'll have sorted out a job that'll keep you interested till, say, half past four. What do you say?'

'I don't know, sir.'

'You say, thank you sir. What do you say?'

'Thank you, sir.'

'I should think so. Now off you go. Fairy rings indeed. What *next*, I ask myself.'

CHAPTER
20

'I can't get over old Blackbum though,' growled Carrie, 'picking on you just because you're a traveller.' The gang was dawdling homeward.

Rosie shook her head. 'It really doesn't matter, Carrie. Mum and Dad move on all the time so I'm never long at one school, except in winter. I don't care what teachers think of me.'

Peter looked at her. 'What *about* winter, Rosie?'

The girl smiled. 'There's this showground near Warwick, with toilets and showers and everything. It's not used in winter so the owner lets us stay there. Not just us, but loads of travellers. It's no fun travelling in the middle of winter, but it's fun at Warwick. We meet up with people we haven't seen all summer. Us kids enrol at the local school on the first of November and leave on the first of April.'

Carrie pulled a face. 'Lucky you. Must feel great, packing up and moving out as soon as the sun shines. *So long everybody – see you in November*. Wish *my* folks were travellers.'

Rosie nodded. 'It *does* feel great, but it's got a downside. No telly for instance.'

'No *telly*?' Carrie sounded horrified.

' 'Course not. We live in an old ambulance.'

'Jeez, I wouldn't be *you*.'

Rosie grinned. 'You just said you wished your folks were travellers.'

'Well yeah, but . . . no *telly*? Phew!'

'There's that,' said Rosie, 'plus sometimes it seems the world's full of people like old Blackbum.'

Peter smiled. 'And Lee Kippax.'

'Yes.' Rosie looked thoughtful. 'I've been thinking about him all day, or rather his dad.'

'His *dad*?' Peter looked baffled. 'Why have you been thinking about *him*, Rosie?

Rosie smiled. 'Remember when old

Massingberd was talking to the nurse, and she said she'd had some guy up to look at her window frames?'

'Yes, I remember.'

'She said his name was Kipper or Kepler, right?'

'Something like that, yes.' Peter looked at her. 'You mean it was . . .?'

'Kippax, of course. He's a joiner, isn't he?'

'Yes, he is. His workshop's near Sizzlers.'

'Right. He's a joiner, and he was up at the Manor inspecting windows. He'd have to go inside to do that, wouldn't he?'

'I guess so.'

'And if there were paintings on the wall he'd see them.'

'I suppose.' His mouth fell open. 'Are you saying . . .?'

'I'm not saying anything, Pete, except old Kippax probably saw those paintings a short time before they were stolen.' She smiled. 'Could be a coincidence, like us arriving at Inchlake just before the burglary. On the other hand . . .'

'On the other hand,' whispered Conrad, 'it might be interesting if a certain bunch of kids went invisible and did a bit of snooping round the Kippax residence.'

Rosie nodded. 'Took the words right out of my mouth, Con. What say we start tonight?'

CHAPTER
21

Twenty past six. Lee Kippax in jeans, T-shirt and trainers stands on the concrete apron in front of his parents' double garage, lobbing shots at the basketball hoop fixed over the door. Neither Foxcroft nor Fairclough have shown up to play with him, and he's bored.

As the bully lobs his forty-eighth shot (nine baskets, thirty-nine misses) something extra-ordinary happens. The ball drops through the bottom of the net but instead of hitting the apron and bouncing, it stops in mid-air. Lee stares at it. The word *hey* falls feebly from his lips. He glances towards the house, hoping his mum's at the window. His mum has already refused to believe he saw a jumper wave at him. *Tiredness*, she says. *Too much television. What you need's a few early nights.* If she was there he'd point. *Look, Mum – is that tiredness? Is it television?* but she's not there. His father's not around either. *Why are grown-ups never around when you want them?*

The ball's still there though, a metre above the ground. Lee stares, hoping there's a thread or something but there isn't. The stupid thing's floating on nothing, like the moon. He tries praying for a witness, but either his prayer goes unheard or the answer's no. He's moistening his top lip with his tongue when the ball chuckles.

What? Laughing at me, is it? Nobody laughs at . . .

'MUM!' Suddenly it's too much and he runs, pelting up the side of the garage. 'MY BALL'S STUCK IN MID-AIR AND IT'S LAUGHING AT ME.'

CHAPTER
22

'*Mum – my ball's stuck in mid-air and it's laughing at me.*' The Invisibles fell about as Conrad ran round the altar stone, pretending to be Kippax. They'd pulled their clothes from the recess and made themselves visible again. It was a breezy evening and they had Inchlake Ring to themselves.

'What a spack,' choked Charlotte. 'His mum'll think he's gone completely bonkers.'

Peter wiped his eyes on a tissue. 'I *loved* the way you caught that ball, Carrie. Lee's face was amazing – like a cartoon. Mind you, we didn't do much snooping.'

Rosie looked at him. 'We probably saw more than you think, Pete.'

'How d'you mean? All we did was spook old Kipper.'

'Ah, but while you were all messing about, I was using my eyes.'

'Oh yeah? And what did you spot, Sherlock?'

Rosie shook her head. 'Never you mind, Pete. I saw what I saw, and I'll tell you all about it when the time's right.' She gazed at the darkening sky. 'I think we'd better go before our folks report us missing.'

As they trudged down the footpath a chill breeze penetrated their T-shirts.

Charlotte shivered. 'There's a touch of autumn in this wind.'

'Don't say *that*,' protested Conrad. 'I want summer to go on for ever so we can keep going invisible. Can you imagine walking about stark naked in the *snow*?'

'Oooh!' Carrie hugged herself. 'It was bad enough tonight, and it's only September. We'll just have to make the most of it while we can and stop for the winter, like we do with rollerblades and biking.'

Rosie smiled. 'You'll be fed up of it by then, anyway.'

'No chance!' Conrad shook his head. 'It's the

coolest thing that's ever happened to me. I'll *never* be fed up.'

'Me neither.' Peter looked at Rosie. '*How* old did you say we'll be when it stops working?'

'Oh – twelve or thirteen. It depends. But as I say, you'll be off it long before then.'

'Not a chance. I'm gonna do it summer *and* winter while I can. I don't want to waste a second.'

It was quite dark when they reached the village outskirts. With brief *goodnights* they separated and four of them hurried towards their homes. The odd one out was Peter. He pretended to head for home, but as soon as the others were out of sight he changed course and walked rapidly towards Inchlake School.

CHAPTER

23

'Oh *there* you are, Rosie.' Daddy Bear was sitting cross-legged by the fire, plaiting strips of leather for a belt. 'We were about to call the police, report you missing.'

Rosie grinned. 'Yeah, right.' She knew he was joking.

'Tea if you want some.' He jerked his head towards the billie in the embers. 'Is anybody coming to this barbie of ours, Friday?'

Rosie poured tea into her mug. 'Oh, yes. Everybody, I think.'

Daddy Bear smiled. 'You mean Miss *Blackburn*'s planning to be here?'

'You know what I mean. All the Invisibles.'

Mummy Bear appeared, carrying a rolled newspaper. 'We thought you'd forgotten where you live, child.' She sat down. 'Any of that tea left?'

Rosie passed the billie. One of the things she liked about her parents was that they hardly ever quizzed her. Most parents would have insisted on knowing where she'd been. She nodded at the newspaper. 'Anything thrilling in there?'

Mummy Bear chuckled. 'Not really, sweetheart. I got it for the burglary, but it doesn't say much.'

'Does it say *gipsies* did it?'

'No, but it says the police are stepping up their inquiries, which probably means we can expect another visit. Tells you what they're looking for, too.'

'Paintings. We knew that already.'

'Yes, but we didn't know *what* paintings. Two Turner seascapes, worth millions.' She smiled. 'You've seen Turners haven't you, Rosie? Fantastic skies, sunlight like some great explosion, gilding everything.' Mummy Bear smiled. 'His dying words were, *The sun is God.*'

Rosie nearly said the Inchlake Invisibles were stepping up their own inquiries. Nearly, but not quite.

CHAPTER
24

Mr Rabbit was irritated. He was supposed to be meeting two guys from work at half past eight, but he didn't dare leave while his wife was in a flap. Mrs Rabbit's flap was due to the fact that Peter wasn't home yet.

'He'll be all right,' soothed Mr Rabbit. 'You know how kids are: they get playing and forget the time.'

'It's easy for you,' snapped his wife. 'All you're bothered about is your silly appointment. He could be floating face-down in the canal or lying somewhere with a broken leg for all you care.'

Peter *wasn't* floating face-down in the canal *or*

lying with a broken leg. He was sitting invisible on the settee, listening to his parents argue. They usually argued when he was in bed, so it was interesting for once to be able to hear what they were saying. Of course he knew it was wrong to eavesdrop, but so what? They'd never know.

'That's not fair, Sue,' protested Mr Rabbit. 'I care about the boy just as much as you do. *More* perhaps, since you'd have preferred a girl.'

Mrs Rabbit glared at her husband. 'Oh that's right – throw *that* in my face again. You're never going to let me forget that, are you?'

Mr Rabbit shrugged. '*You* brought up the subject of caring, Sue, not me. All I'm saying . . .'

The row grew more heated but Peter wasn't following it now. He was staring horrified at his mother while a stricken voice inside his head whimpered, *You didn't want me, you wanted a girl. You're my mum, but I could walk out of here right now and never come back and you wouldn't even care.*

His father was pacing the room, looking at his watch. His mother, her face like thunder, lifted a corner of the curtain and tutted, letting it fall. They were waiting for him, but not because they cared. He was spoiling their evening, that's all.

INVISIBLE!

They hated him. He could see it in their faces. He got up and crept from the room, fighting the aching lump in his throat.

If someone's invisible, can you see their tears?

CHAPTER
25

'Lee?'

The boy was hanging about near the teachers' car park, looking miserable. He turned as Rosie spoke his name. 'What do *you* want, gipsy?'

'Just to talk.'

'What about?'

'About what you saw yesterday, on the field.'

'Oh yeah? What about it?'

'I want you to know you're not going crazy, that's all.'

'Crazy? *I* know I'm not going crazy. What makes you think I think I'm going crazy?'

Rosie gazed at him. 'You weren't looking too happy just now, Lee, and it *can* be a bit of a shock, seeing somebody vanish. And you *did* see it, that's what I wanted to say. It's a sort of trick I do, so like, you don't need a doctor or anything.'

He scowled at her. 'How about telling The Bee all this. And my dad.'

'No way. This is strictly a kid thing. No adults. If you tell anyone I'll just deny it.'

'Uh . . . I don't suppose . . . you weren't around *my* place last night, by any chance?'

Rosie grinned. 'Funny you should say that, Lee.'

'Why – *were* you?'

'Of course. Balls don't *really* hang in mid-air, do they? And they certainly don't laugh.'

The boy goggled. 'That was *you*? *Really?*' Hope in his voice, and the very beginning of joy.

'Sure it was.' She chuckled. 'I thought you said you weren't worried.'

'Yeah, well . . .' He looked uncomfortable. 'It's . . . you know . . . the way nobody believes you. You *know* you saw what you saw, but everybody's giving you funny looks and after a bit you start thinking, *Did I see it, or am I going round the twist?* It's scary.'

'Well you can quit worrying, and you can tell

Lee and Carl to chill out too, only don't try telling any grown-ups because they won't believe a word.' She winked. 'See you, apple-thief.'

'Hang on.' He looked at her. 'This trick of yours. You wouldn't ... I mean ... how about teaching me, huh? There's a million ways I could use a trick like that.'

She nodded. 'I just bet there are, and I can imagine what some of them would be, too.' She shook her head. 'Sorry, Lee. You're just not ready for that sort of responsibility. See you later.'

CHAPTER
26

'Good day, sweetheart?'

Rosie stowed her bag in the miniature cupboard under her bed. When your home's that small you've got to be tidy. She smiled up at Mummy Bear. 'Not bad. You?'

'Terrific. Sold a dozen belts and took orders for another dozen, didn't we, Daddy?'

'Sure did.' Daddy Bear grinned. 'Inchlake's crazy for hand-crafted leather.'

'Does this mean we can afford some Chinese takeaway for supper, Dad?'

'Oh, I think we might stretch to it . . . but only if you talked to Lee Kippax.'

Rosie nodded. 'I did. Told him to stop worrying.'

'And what did he say?'

'Oh, he tried to pretend he wasn't bothered but he was *really* relieved. You could tell.'

'I'm not surprised, sweetheart. It can't be much fun, wondering if you're losing your marbles. So you're friends now, are you?'

'I wouldn't say that, no.' She grinned. 'He wanted me to teach him the trick. Said there were a million ways he could use it.'

'And what did you say?'

'I told him he wasn't ready for the responsibility.'

Daddy Bear gazed at his daughter. 'And what about yourself, Rosie? Will *you* be a little more responsible from now on? No more driving bullies bonkers as a way of getting even?'

The girl blushed. 'I won't do that again, Daddy Bear. Promise.'

'Even when they call you thief or gipsy?'

'Even when they call me thief or gipsy.'

He nodded. 'Good. So, who fancies what from the Chinese chippy?'

CHAPTER 27

They'd polished off their chicken fried rice and were munching prawn crackers when they heard a car.

'Hey up.' Daddy Bear got to his feet, looking towards the sound. 'Police I expect, stepping up their inquiries.'

It wasn't the police. It was a man in a suit, looking pretty upset. Daddy Bear gazed at him. He'd never seen him before.

'Can I help you?'

The man was glancing this way and that, as though looking for somebody. He saw Rosie by the fire. 'Are you at the local school – Miss Blackburn's class?'

Rosie swallowed a cheekful of cracker and nodded. 'Yes I am.'

'So you'll know Peter – Peter Rabbit?'

She nodded again. 'He's my friend.'

Mummy Bear stood up. 'What's this about, Mr . . .?'

'Rabbit. I'm Peter's father. He didn't come home after school today. His mother's frantic. We wondered if he was here.'

'Well no, Mr Rabbit, I'm afraid we've not seen him. Have you told the police?'

'It was the first thing we did, but you know what they're like. *Shouldn't worry, sir, he'll show up at bedtime. They usually do.* It's all right for them. They don't have Mrs Rabbit to cope with.'

'No.' Mummy Bear looked at Rosie. 'Did you talk to Peter at school today, sweetheart?'

'Yes, of course.'

'And did he seem OK? I mean, not worried or anything?'

'He was a bit quieter than usual, I suppose.'

'But he didn't mention going anywhere after school?'

'No.'

Daddy Bear looked at Mr Rabbit. 'Why don't you sit down a minute, have a cup of tea? You look just about jiggered. We'll clear away, then take the van out and help you search. How's that sound?'

The man nodded. 'I could murder a cuppa now you come to mention it, and I don't suppose a few minutes'll make much difference. Thanks.' He sat down on the grass. Daddy Bear poured tea from the billie into a mug and handed it to him. Mr Rabbit sipped gratefully as the three travellers cleared up the remains of their supper and damped down the fire. It was seven o'clock and quite dark when the two vehicles swung out onto the road and growled off in opposite directions, going slowly.

Rosie pressed her face to the glass, peering out, thinking, *I hope the daft beggar's not gone invisible or there's no chance.* She turned to Mummy Bear. 'Go towards Inchlake Ring, Mum. I want to check something out.'

CHAPTER

28

Peter wasn't invisible, but tramping a country lane between high hedges at two in the morning he was pretty hard to see. Not that there was anyone to see him. The road from Inchlake to Sowerby isn't used much at night, and if he heard a vehicle he'd duck down in the ditch till it passed.

Sowerby was where Peter's grandma lived. Grandma Fox, not Grandma Rabbit. There was this family joke about Mum and Dad. Something about a rabbit catching a fox. The grown-ups laughed about it at parties but Peter thought it was daft, and he certainly wasn't in the mood for it tonight. *Shame the rabbit didn't* miss *the flipping fox*, he thought savagely, *then I'd never have been born and everybody'd be better off.* He was feeling really really sorry for himself.

It'll be OK at Grandma's. She likes me if nobody else does. She'll do me hot milk and biscuits and I'll tell her what they said. I'll ask her to let me sleep over, and not to phone Mum and Dad till tomorrow. That'll teach 'em. They'll be worried sick, even though they don't care about me really. They've always been funny about me being out after dark. He smiled to himself. *Two o'clock and they won't even be in bed. They'll stay up all night and be shattered tomorrow and it'll serve 'em right.*

He was so wrapped up in his thoughts that when a van came nosing out of a gateway he was crossing, he had to fling himself backwards to keep from being hit. He hadn't noticed the gateway or heard the van, which was travelling without lights. His violent evasive action dumped him on the seat of his pants and he sat dazed as the vehicle swung left and roared away, still without lights. *Didn't even see me*, he thought, picking himself up. *Good mind to report him, except I'd need his number and I didn't get it.* He'd noticed *something* though. Something familiar. As he knocked dirt off the seat of his jeans with both hands he realized he'd seen the van before, loads of times, but what the heck was it doing coming out of someone's driveway without lights at two o'clock in the morning? He shook his head, too tired to think about it now. Sowerby seemed pretty close when you went by car, but it was turning out to be quite a hike. He yawned and plodded on.

CHAPTER
29

'Peter Rabbit.' Miss Blackburn glanced up from her register. 'Anybody know where Peter is?'

'Miss.' Rosie held up her hand. 'He went missing, miss. Last night. His dad came to where we're parked and we went looking, but we didn't find him. I think Mr Beecroft knows about it, miss.'

A buzz went round the classroom. Lee Kippax scribbled something on a bit of paper and slipped it to Carl Foxcroft. The note passed from hand to hand till it reached Rosie. She smoothed it out and read: *What happened, gipsy? Trick go wrong, did it? What if I grass you up?* She turned the paper over and wrote, *One word from you, and stuff will happen that'll make the laughing ball seem normal. Keep it zipped, apple-thief.* She watched the boy's face turn pale as he read. He wasn't going to say a single word.

The twins found her at break-time.

'When did he *go*, Rosie? He was with us, walking home.'

'I know, but he never arrived. Must've gone off after we split up.'

'D'you think it's got something to do with . . . you know?'

Rosie shrugged. 'Maybe. His stuff wasn't up the Ring though – I checked.'

'What about *there*?' Carrie nodded towards the far corner of the field.

'No. I looked before school.'

'That leaves the ice house.'

Rosie shook her head. 'I don't think he's gone invisible. He's run off, that's all.'

Conrad pulled a face. 'Or someone's taken him. It happens.'

'Yes well . . . we've just got to hope it didn't happen this time.'

Halfway through lunch, Peter walked into the yard. Rosie and the twins ran to him. 'What *happened*, Pete? Where've you *been*?' He looked pale, but otherwise fine.

'I ... I've been at my gran's. Bit of hassle at home. Ran off.'

'What sort of hassle?'

'I don't feel like talking about it, OK?'

'Sure. Sorted now, though?'

Peter shrugged. 'I guess. Listen.' He looked at Rosie. 'I saw something funny last night.'

'What?'

'Lee's dad's van, coming out of a driveway on the Sowerby road.'

'What's funny about *that*, Pete?'

'Two in the morning, no lights. Practically ran me over.'

'Hmm.' Rosie grinned. 'Maybe old Kippax has a girlfriend out that way.'

'Maybe. I thought I'd mention it, that's all.'

She nodded. 'Glad you did. Good to have you back, too. We thought you'd been murdered.'

Peter smiled wanly. 'I nearly was, by my gran. Half two, I got to her place. She goes, *Do your parents know where you are?* I say, *No, I want them to worry*, and she goes mental. Yells at me, phones them. I get to sleep over, but Mum comes for me at half eight. Nice as pie in front of

Gran but goes ape-shape in the car. Can't say I feel like school.'

Rosie shook her head. 'Don't blame you. Take it easy, that's all. Don't do too much, and it'll be half three before you know it.'

'Oh goody, then I can go home and have Dad yell at me. Can't wait.'

'Could be worse though, Pete. Could be floating face-down in the canal or lying somewhere with a broken leg.'

Peter stared at her. 'That's exactly what . . . you weren't at *my* place last night, were you? Invisible, I mean. Around eight?'

'What are you, *crazy*? Why would I . . . ?'

'I dunno.' He shook his head. 'Maybe I *am* crazy. I *feel* it. Everything seems . . .' His face crumpled. He bowed his head into cupped hands and cried so hard his body shook.

CHAPTER
30

Three forty-five. Rosie arrived home to find a police car parked behind the old ambulance. It was drizzling so there was no fire and nobody outside. The rear doors stood open. She mounted the step and looked in. Her parents and the two officers, sitting on chairs and bunks, practically filled the place.

Mummy Bear smiled. 'Come on in, sweetheart. Room for a little one.' She budged up and Rosie sat beside her on the bunk, hugging her bag.

One of the officers was talking to Daddy Bear. 'Before, you said you were here last night. Now you say you were out searching for some kid. Which is true?'

Daddy Bear sighed. 'I thought you meant like, late. We *were* out earlier, looking for Peter Rabbit.'

The officer gazed at the big traveller through narrowed eyes. 'I hope you're not pulling my leg, sir, because this is no joking matter.'

'I'm not pulling your leg. What makes you think I am?'

'Oh come *on*, sir. Daddy Bear, Mummy Bear, and now Peter Rabbit. Where'd you find the kid – on Mr McGregor's carrot patch?'

'We didn't find him at all. You should be out looking for him now, instead of harrassing innocent citizens.'

'He's turned up,' interrupted Rosie. 'He was at his gran's.'

The officer nodded. 'They usually are, love.' He turned back to Daddy Bear. 'So that's why you were seen driving along the Sowerby Road at eight-fifteen last night – you were looking for Peter Rabbit?'

'Not me, Sergeant. That'd be my wife and young Rosie. I was with the kid's dad in his car.'

'I see. And the only thing you were interested in last night was finding Peter Rabbit?'

'That's correct.'

'So the name Sowerby Old Hall means nothing to you?'

'Sowerby Old Hall? Not a thing, Sergeant. Should it?'

'That rather depends, sir.'

'On what?'

'On whether you're fond of ancient Greek sculpture. Fond enough to nick a three thousand-year-old life-size bronze statue of Poseidon from the middle of an ornamental pond.'

Daddy Bear pulled a face. 'Ancient Greek sculpture? I can take it or leave it, Sergeant. Mostly I leave it, because as you see . . .' He indicated the snug compartment with a sweep of his brawny arm. 'We don't have a lot of room here for life-size statues, of Poseidon or anybody else.' He grinned. 'Of course you're welcome to search the place if you suspect the thing's cunningly concealed behind a false wall or something. Far be it from me to obstruct a police officer in the execution of his duty.'

'Very droll, sir, I'm sure.' The sergeant stood up. 'We'll be on our way.' He smiled tightly. 'Wouldn't want to keep you because you never know – you might have to go out looking for Noddy or somebody. G'night, sir.'

CHAPTER
31

Rosie got up and followed the officers out.

'Excuse me?'

'What is it, miss?'

'Sowerby Old Hall. Has it got like a gateway in a high hedge so if you were walking you wouldn't see a car coming out till it was practically on top of you?'

'It might have. Why? Been there, have you?'

'N-no. We might have passed it last night though, me and Mum.'

'Very likely, if you were on the Sowerby road. See anything suspicious, did you? Loiterers, parked motor?'

'No. We were looking for . . .'

'I know. Peter Rabbit. Listen. If you do see or hear anything, you'll be sure and let us know, won't you?'

''Course I will. G'night.'

'OK if I go out after tea, Mum?'

Mummy Bear was mashing potatoes while her husband set the table. She nodded. 'I suppose so, sweetheart, but it's not a very nice evening. Something important to do, have you?'

'I think so, yes. I'll try not to be late.'

By six o'clock it was windy as well as wet. She didn't fancy the climb to Inchlake Ring so she used the fairy ring on the school field, packing her clothes in a plastic carrier bag which she hid in the long grass, weighted down with a stone. It would be dark soon, and it was unlikely that anyone would visit the field tonight.

The wind drove a cold drizzle that plastered her hair to her scalp and made her shiver as she hurried towards the Kippax home. This was why she'd decided not to involve the others – they'd have been half-frozen and ready to give up before the job was done.

The place was in darkness. No car stood on

the drive. When the security floodlight snapped on in response to Rosie's movements, the ring of raindrops round the basketball hoop became a circlet of diamonds. The light didn't worry her. In fact it made her task much easier, and if some busybody neighbour wondered what had triggered it and came to take a peek, he'd see nothing. *If old Kippax had a guard dog instead of a floodlight,* she thought, *it would be a different story.*

She circled the house, triggering another light round the back. There was a garden shed with a window in the side. She wiped off rainbeads and peered in. The light helped, but the shed held only a clothes-spinner, some tools and a motor mower. No life-size statue of Poseidon. *Who the heck's Poseidon anyway?*

She tried to see into the house, but all the curtains were drawn. That left the garage. The double garage. *Plenty of space in there, but no window. Drat!*

She was standing, shivering a bit and wondering what to do, when she heard a car approaching. Powerful headlights slashed across the driveway as a BMW turned in. Rosie sidestepped as the car came growling up the drive, and seized the opportunity to peer inside

286

the garage when its doors swung up auto-
matically and the headlights illuminated the
interior. She glimpsed a tall, angular object
draped in a shroud of shiny black plastic like a
giant bin-bag. *That could be a statue*, she told herself. *A life-size statue. It's Daddy Bear's height. A
peek under that plastic's what I need. Just a peek.*

She wasn't going to get it though. As she
stared, the car rolled into the garage and the
door began to swing down behind it. If there'd
been time to think, she wouldn't have done the
crazy thing she now did, but there wasn't. The
door was half down when she dashed forward,
ducked, scuttled under the descending rim and
jumped clear. As the garage door clicked shut,
the car doors opened and three people got out.
She was trapped with the family Kippax.

CHAPTER
32

'Are we watching *The Simpsons*, Mum?' Lee hovered by the door which led from the garage to the house as his parents unloaded the car.

'You can watch in your room. Your dad's got somebody coming in a few minutes.'

'Who?'

'Never you mind. Here – take these through.'

Lee took two bulging carriers from his mother. 'Who's coming? Why can't I see 'em?'

'Lee.' Mr Kippax frowned at his son. 'Don't argue with your mother, OK? Put that stuff in the kitchen and go upstairs.'

'Yes, Dad.'

Lee went through the door. Rosie, motionless

against a breeze-block wall, watched as Mr and
Mrs Kippax picked up their stuff and followed
him. Should she go too, or stay here? Would
they lock the door and if they did, was there a
way she could escape once she'd seen what was
under that plastic?

*I've got to stay, haven't I? Take a peek in the bin-
bag,* then *worry about getting out.* Laden with
carriers, Mr Kippax followed his wife through
the door and pushed it closed with his bottom.
Rosie heard a latch click home, and at the same
instant the garage was plunged into total darkness.

*Drat! Never thought of that. No window. Can't see
a hand in front of my face. Don't know where the
switches are. Why didn't I bring a* torch, *for Pete's
sake? (Because it'd look a bit funny, that's why – a
torch floating along the street all by itself.) Still, I
should've been prepared in some way.*

Gotta do *something. Can't just stand here freezing. Move.* Where, *though?* She frowned in the
blackness, trying to remember the layout of the
place. There was a board. Pegboard painted
white with tools racked up on it, somewhere to
her right. Under the board was a bench with a
vice and a power-drill. Shelves below, full of

stuff. A lamp, perhaps. A torch. Matches would do. *Have to search by feel but that's OK – I've probably got all night.*

She crabbed right, keeping the breeze-blocks at her back. *Go slow. Don't trip. Don't knock anything over.* When she thought she'd travelled far enough she raised her right arm and felt for the board. It wasn't there. *On a bit, then. Slowly, slowly. Now, try again. Nothing. It's here somewhere though, unless I imagined it. Wish Daddy Bear was here. Shut up. There – I've found it. Smooth and cool, just like me. Now for the bench . . . there. And underneath, down here somewhere . . . all sorts of rubbish. Careful then. Lift things one by one, feel 'em, put them on the floor. That way you won't be looking at the same stuff twice. Looking at! If only.*

Time passed. She couldn't identify most of the items her groping hands found, but none of them was a torch or lamp. She'd cleared the top shelf and made a start on the lower one when she heard a click. The lights came on. Mr Kippax, in the doorway, growled an oath as he spotted the stuff on the floor. Rosie shrank away as he strode towards her, murder in his eyes.

CHAPTER
33

Lee laughed out loud and slapped his knees as Bart Simpson pulled down his jeans and mooned the Prime Minister of Australia while a band somewhere struck up *The Star-Spangled Banner*. *Mega! Way to go, Bart. Best episode ever, this.*

'Lee!'

Oh-oh. 'Yes, Dad?'

'I'll give you "yes dad". Get down here *now.*'

Oh heck – now what have I done? 'Coming, Dad.'

'What you been playing at, eh?'

Lee gaped at the stuff all over the garage floor. 'Wasn't *me*, Dad. Never left my room.'

'Don't lie to me, boy.'

'I'm not. I haven't been in here, Dad. Honest.'

'So who *did* this? Your *mother*? The Invisible *Man*?'

'I dunno, Dad, but it wasn't me.'

'Oh, wasn't it? Well I'll tell you one thing – it's *you*'s going to put it all back, and you'd better be quick about it. I've somebody coming any minute and he'll not see *my* place looking like a tip. Go on – get it sorted before I kick your backside.'

Not fair. On his knees on the concrete floor, stacking stuff under the bench while *The Simpsons* performed to his empty room. *Why do I always get the blame?* He wished he had Bart's guts. He'd run through to the kitchen where Dad was putting the kettle on for his visitor, drop his jeans and moon the miserable so-and-so. Better, he'd wait till the mysterious visitor was actually *here*, drinking tea in the front room, and do it to the pair of them. Yeah, *that*'s what old Bart'd do. *Who did this, though? Somebody must have. It wasn't like this when we got back from Safeways. What if somebody broke in? Is still here?* He glanced around, moistening his lips with his tongue, but the garage was brilliantly lit. No murky corners, except . . .

He gazed towards the angular object under its black shroud. *Could be hiding under there with whatever it is.* Trouble was, he didn't dare go look. Not because he was scared of what he might find, but because he was scared of his father. *What's under that sheeting's none of your business, boy. Understand?* He'd said that months ago, when the first mysterious shape had appeared, and Lee knew he meant it. It wasn't the actual words so much as the dangerous light in the man's eyes as he spoke them. Lee knew that light. The black sheeting had covered many an intriguing item since then and Lee had stayed well clear. You didn't mess with Bob Kippax when he got that light in his eye.

The Invisible Man. Lee drew in a sharp breath, peering about him. *What if . . . ?* He moistened his lips again and croaked, 'Rosie? Rosie Walk, are you here? Did *you* do this? Say something, for Pete's sake.'

No, don't.

CHAPTER
34

Rosie stood beside the statue of Poseidon, holding her breath till Lee decided she wasn't there and went back to stacking away the stuff she'd got out. Now the lights were on she could see she'd groped in vain. There was no flashlight. No matches.

It *was* a statue. She'd lifted a corner of the giant bin-bag while Lee was busy and seen a greenish foot and the shaft of what might be a spear. She didn't know for sure it was Poseidon, but it'd be a strange coincidence if it was some other statue after Peter's midnight encounter with Kippax's van in the gateway of Sowerby Old Hall.

So I was right. Kippax senior's our thief. I bet he lifted those two Turners from Inchlake Manor too. So. All I have to do is get out of here, go visible and tell the police. That'll teach 'em – case solved by prime suspect. Prime suspect's kid anyway.

Her train of thought was derailed by the sound of a motor. Lee shot a glance towards the garage door and began to work faster, but the door to the house opened and his father strode through.

'Leave that now. Go to your room and stay there till I say you can come out. Move.'

Lee straightened up, scuttled past his father and vanished into the house. *Maybe I should follow,* thought Rosie, but old Kippax moved to a box on the wall and thumbed a green button. The garage door swung up. Rosie grinned. *Panic over. I can leave now whenever I want to.*

Under the floodlight stood a van. It had reversed up the driveway. Now it came scrunching into the garage. It wasn't the blue Kippax van which had nearly squashed Pete. This one was red, and pretty ancient. Rosie tiptoed over to the house door so she could watch and not be in the way.

Two men got out.

'Bit late,' growled Kippax. 'Thought you'd blobbed.'

The driver shrugged. 'Traffic, squire. God!' He'd spotted the bin-bag. 'I'd have hired a ruddy elephant if I'd known it was this size. Solid bronze and all.'

Kippax shook his head. 'Hollow. Just over a tonne. Piece of cake, *and* you get a cuppa when it's loaded. Not many people'd look after you like I do.' He went across and started ripping away the polythene. The driver and his mate joined in. In seconds the statue stood revealed – six feet of gleaming muscle wearing a crown of seaweed and brandishing a trident, his feet buried in a drift of torn plastic. Rosie nodded to herself. *Of course. Poseidon's another name for Father Neptune and here he is, folks. Why doesn't somebody pass by right now and spot him?* She slitted her eyes, peering down the floodlit driveway. *Oh, right. Hidden by the van. Crafty swines. I wonder . . . can I get to school, go visible, run to the police station and get back here in a patrol car before they load up, drink their tea and drive away?*

I can give it a flipping good try.

CHAPTER
35

'Now then, miss, what can we do for you?'

'I need to speak to Detective Sergeant Springer. It's urgent.'

'Oh, aye?' The constable scrutinized Rosie from rat-tail hair to sodden trainers. 'You look half-frozen. Are you all right?'

'I'm fine. Look – I know where that statue is but they're shifting it. It'll be gone in a few minutes.'

'Statue?'

'Yes, you know. The Greek one. Poseidon, from Sowerby Old Hall. Sergeant Springer questioned my dad about it, said I was to let him know if I saw anything.'

The constable pulled a fat ledger towards him and picked up a pen. 'Can I have your name, miss? Name and address.'

'Rosie. Rosie Walk. We're travellers, parked on that bit of the old Cleeston road by Inchlake Woods.'

'Aah, right.' The officer nodded. 'You're one of the Three Bears, aren't you?' He smiled. 'Baby Bear, I suppose. Well, Baby Bear, I'm afraid Sergeant Springer's not on duty tonight. Comes on at eight tomorrow morning. You could try then.'

'Tomorrow *morning*?' Rosie was outraged. 'That statue's being loaded on a van *now*. It could be in Timbuctoo by morning. Let me talk to whoever's on duty.'

'*I'm* on duty, miss. Constable Stables. Talk to me.'

'I *have*, but you don't seem to believe me.'

'That's because you haven't given me much to go on, miss. Where exactly *is* this statue, and how come *you* know about it?'

'It's in Mr Kippax's garage, and I know because I was there. I saw it.'

'Mr Kippax's garage?' The constable gazed at her. 'D'you mean *Bob* Kippax, the joiner?'

'Yes. His son's in the same class as me.'

'Is he now? And what were you doing up there, miss? It's a long way from the woods.'

'I was . . . investigating.'

'Investigating? Playing at private detectives, you mean?'

'No, I wasn't *playing*. Mr Kippax was up Inchlake Manor just before those paintings were taken, *and* his van was seen near Sowerby Old Hall last night.'

'Seen?' The constable stared at her. 'By *who*, may I ask?'

'It's *whom*.'

'What?'

'You say *whom*, not *who*. And it was Peter Rabbit.'

'Peter Rabbit.' He sighed. 'You're sure it was Peter Rabbit *whom* saw this van, and not Squirrel Nutkin or Bart Simpson or Alice in Wonderland?'

'Peter Rabbit's *real*. He's in . . .'

'Don't tell me. The same class as you, right?'

'Yes.'

The officer sighed again. 'Listen, miss. I don't know if you've heard, but there's a crime wave all over the country. The police are pretty stretched trying to cope with the genuine stuff. What we *don't* need is a lot of hassle from kids called things like Baby Bear and Peter Rabbit, with overdeveloped imaginations and too little to do. And now I'll have to ask you to run along, because I'm very busy. G'night, miss.'

CHAPTER
36

'Hi, Pete. All right?' Thursday morning, just before the buzzer.

Peter nodded. 'Not bad, thanks.'

Rosie smiled. 'For someone who nearly got run over by thieves, eh?'

'How d'you mean, thieves?'

'The place you were passing when the van nearly got you was Sowerby Old Hall, right?'

'I haven't a clue.'

'Well it was. And that same night, by a strange coincidence, a statue was pinched from the grounds of Sowerby Old Hall. And by an even stranger coincidence, that statue later showed up in old Kippax's garage.'

The boy goggled. 'How the heck do you *know* all this, Rosie?'

She told him about Sergeant Springer's visit to her home, and her own to the Kippax residence. She was explaining how she'd got herself locked in the garage when Carrie and Conrad joined them and she had to start all over again.

When she'd finished, Carrie said, 'Why didn't you *tell* us you were investigating? We could have come with you. We're supposed to be a gang, you know.'

'I know and I meant to, but it was so *cold*. You'd have hated it.'

'*You* managed.'

'I'm used to it. Thing is what do we *do*, now the police don't believe us?'

Conrad looked at her. 'They didn't believe *you*, Rosie, 'cause you're a stranger and a traveller. If one of *us* had been there . . .'

'It'd have made no difference,' interrupted his twin. 'It's not because Rosie's a stranger *or* a traveller, it's because she's a kid. Haven't you noticed grown-ups *never* believe kids?'

Conrad pulled a face. ''Course I have, turkey.

So what do we do?'

'Get evidence. Hey Rosie – I've got a camera. Why don't we go up the Kippax place tonight and take a picture of the statue? *That*'d prove you weren't lying, wouldn't it?'

Rosie sighed and shook her head. 'It's *gone*, Carrie. I told you, a van came for it.'

'Oh, yeah. Well – couldn't we grab Lee? Force him to confess?'

'Sure, if you fancy a rumble with Rex Fairclough and Carl Foxcroft. *I* don't.'

'Hey, have you noticed,' said Conrad, 'they've all got the letter X in their names? Kippax, Rex, Foxcroft? D'you think that's why they're a gang?'

His sister snorted. 'What the X has *that* got to do with anything, you dummy?'

'I just noticed, that's all.'

'We've got a choice,' murmured Rosie. 'Either we find a way of making someone believe us, or we say it's none of our business and stop being invisible detectives.'

Carrie shook her head. 'We can't do *that*, Rosie. It's against the law to know about a crime and not tell the police, and we know about a crime *and* who did it. We've *got* to do something. Question is, what?'

The buzzer sounded as she spoke, and Rosie pulled a face. 'We'll talk about it tomorrow,' she said, 'at the barbie.'

CHAPTER
37

Three thirty-five. The twins, walking home.

'Hey, Con?'

'What?'

'Old Kippax. He's got that yard near Sizzlers, right?'

''Course. What about it?'

'Well, we've investigated his house but not the yard. It's piled up with all sorts of junk, and then there's the buildings. He could hide a flipping *elephant* there and nobody'd know.'

'There's no elephants missing.'

'You know what I mean, dummy. Those paintings might be there. I reckon we ought to take a peek.'

'You could be right. Mention it to Rosie tomorrow night.'

Carrie shook her head. 'I'm not talking about Rosie, Con. I'm talking about you and me. What's wrong with the two of us taking a look by ourselves?'

Conrad looked at her. 'You mean like, go invisible without Rosie? Or would we do it visible?'

'Invisible, you donkey. We'll use Inchlake Ring. It'll work just the same without Rosie.'

'Yeah I know, but like . . . I prefer to have her around in case something goes wrong.'

'Like *what*, for Pete's sake?'

'Well, like if we went invisible and couldn't get back. You know – walked round the ring and just stayed invisible?'

'It won't happen, and if it did I don't suppose there's anything Rosie could do about it. I say we do it today, straight after tea.'

'I'd want to think about it first.'

'Chicken.'

'It's not that. I just don't like rushing into stuff.'

'Chicken.'

'Shut your face.'

'Chicken. I'll go by myself.'

'You can't.'

'What'll you do, chicken-licken – tell Mummy?'

'No.'

'Keep me in an armlock all night?'

'Don't be daft.'

'Come with me then.'

'I . . . oh, what the heck. All *right*, but don't blame me if we both end up invisible for ever.'

Carrie grinned. 'You're a hero, Con. I always said so.'

CHAPTER
38

It was dry, but a spiteful wind whipped the bleached grass round the feet of the ancient stones and drove flocks of ragged clouds across the sky. Conrad shivered.

'Flipping freezing.'

His twin nodded. 'Wait till you've no clothes on.'

'Oooh, don't. Think I'll go invisible first, *then* strip off.'

'Good idea.' There was nobody about. The pair positioned themselves and began walking backwards. '*Does* feel strange without Rosie. You were right about that.'

'Want to change your mind?'

'You wish!'

They completed the circle. Conrad looked down at himself. 'Think it's worked?'

''Course it has, you turkey. Let's get our stuff off. It'll be dark in an hour.'

'You start. I'm just going to take my clothes for a walk.'

'What's the point? There's nobody to see.'

'I don't care. I'll *pretend* there's someone. The Bee.'

'You're a nut.'

Carrie crossed to the stone with the recess, unzipping her top. She was shrugging it off when she heard a cry. Turning, she saw her brother topple backwards, arms flailing. She was about to laugh, but then the back of his head struck the altar stone with a sound like an apple splitting. He slumped sideways and lay like a rag doll, one arm cocked against the sky.

'Con? Conrad?' She ran towards him, her top flapping. He didn't move. She knelt, feeling his brow. 'Con? Are you OK? *Say* something.' *Daft stuff you come out with when you're scared.* 'Con?' *Shake him. No, don't. Not supposed to move someone who's had an accident, right?* She wished she knew first aid, not just fragments picked up from the

309

telly. *He's knocked out. Dead, maybe. What the heck do I do?*

Fetch someone. Go visible first, of course, then find an adult. Or a house with a phone. Yeah, that's it. A house with a phone. Ambulance. We were playing. Just playing, and my brother overbalanced. I'll say that to Josh, like on Casualty. *He'll know exactly what to do. Clear the airway. Immobilize the head. All that. Yeah, but . . .*

Invisible. *She* could go visible in a minute, but what about him? *She* could see him, but to anybody else there'd just be a set of clothes. What would she tell Josh about that? *Oh yes, he's invisible at the moment. We go invisible sometimes. There* is *a head though, somewhere, and it's bleeding . . .*

Impossible. Can't fetch help and don't have a clue what to do myself. One thing. One possibility. If I carry him round the ring he'll go visible, won't he? Or have you got to be awake? Can but try. Then if it works I can get somebody. I know they say don't move the patient, but . . .

'Come on, Con love. Up we go.'

CHAPTER
39

It was unbelievably difficult. Flopping and lolling, the helpless Conrad felt like a tonne of mutton. It took Carrie more than a minute to drag him backwards, heels trailing, to the edge of the ring. She kept expecting somebody to show up and see her apparently struggling with a very heavy set of clothes. *What the heck am I gonna say? Oh, I just thought I'd take this stuff to the Oxfam shop but I seem to have come the wrong way.* Yeah, sure.

It was when she started trying to move the unconscious boy *forward* that it got really hard. She couldn't hook her hands under his armpits and drag him like before, because they'd both be going backwards. She had to sit him facing forward, then haul him to his feet and sort of *push* him in front of her. His head rolled to and fro on his chest, his arms waved about and his feet kept getting tangled up with hers. She couldn't do it in one go, it was far too tiring. Every few metres she'd stop, let him slide down till he was sitting, and squat behind him panting for a few seconds, her head on his shoulder. *What if it doesn't work – if you've got to do it non-stop?* It was no use thinking about that, or about the harm she might be doing by lugging him about. Somebody could turn up at any minute.

She'd forgotten where she'd started, so it was only the appearance of their faint shadows on the ground which told her she'd succeeded. She'd carried him right round, and it had worked. They were visible. She glanced at her watch. Five past seven. It had taken her nearly twenty minutes. Her twin was still unconscious but she could feel him breathing, which was a relief. Now she must leave him and seek help, though she was exhausted enough to fall down on the grass and sleep. She cradled his head and gazed into the pale, still face. 'Con, I've got to

leave you now, get help. You'll be OK, won't
you, till I get back?'

There was a farm just off the footpath near the
bottom of the hill. A farm*house* anyway – it
wasn't a working farm any more, but the people
would have a phone. She paused between two
great stones, glanced back at the small figure in
the grass, then started running. The sun was
setting over her left shoulder. Soon it would be
dark.

Carriage lamps mounted either side of the
door came on as she slammed the knocker.
Footsteps beyond the iron-studded door, which
opened on a chain. A slice of face in the gap.

'Yes?'

'Please can I use your phone? My brother's
had an accident, up the Ring.'

'What sort of accident? You're not doing
drugs or anything, are you?'

'No. We were playing and he fell. Hit his head
on a stone. He's knocked out.'

'OK, just a sec.'

There were three people. One woman, two
men. They sat her down, fetched her tea while
one man phoned. She wrapped her hands round
the hot beaker and stared into the fire. She

hadn't noticed till now how cold she was. The warmth was making her drowsy.

The ambulance came in fifteen minutes and she had to go out, get boosted into the high cab, show the way. It wasn't Josh; it was two women. When the headlights hit the standing stones it was nearly dark. Con didn't seem to have moved. They piled out. The women, herself, one of the men from the farm. The women bent over her brother. One of them said, 'Conrad, can you hear me? Can you say something? It's all right. You're going to be fine.'

They stretchered him into the ambulance, which bounced down the path, stopping briefly to let the man off at the house. Carrie nodded. 'Thanks.' She was scared for Con, but half asleep too. She hardly noticed when the vehicle reached the road and accelerated. The siren stitched a thin blue thread of light across her dream.

CHAPTER 40

As the twins were being rushed to hospital, a really terrific idea popped into Charlotte's head. She hadn't seen the others for a few days and was sitting on her bed, wondering whether they were having invisible adventures without her. She could hear a siren somewhere in the distance. *Some poor soul off to hospital, God love 'em. I could go to school invisible.*

Just like that. What an ambulance siren had to do with going to school invisible she'd never know but that's how it happened, and the more she thought about it the more fun it promised to be. In fact she hardly slept that night, she was so excited. Friday morning she left home half an hour early and went the long way round so she'd pass Inchlake School. The yard was still deserted so she ran onto the field. The ring of little toadstools was exactly where Rosie had told her it was. She stepped in, walked carefully backwards and went invisible. Undressing quickly, she checked to see she was casting no shadow. Then she stuffed her clothes in her sports bag and hurried to the hawthorn hedge which bordered part of the field. Kids were drifting into the yard. She put the bag down, kicked it right under and piled dead leaves and rubbish in front of it. When she was satisfied it wouldn't be seen she straightened up and strolled back, wondering what the kids would think if they knew there was a girl with nothing on in their midst.

She arrived at Holy Family with ten minutes to spare. It was great, loitering by groups of her classmates, earwigging. Just before nine Teresa Walsh said, 'Hey – anyone seen Spider?' Spider was Charlotte's nickname. Then the bell rang.

'Charlotte Webb?' Ms Weekes was doing the register. She looked up. 'Anybody seen Charlotte this morning?'

'No, miss.'

'No, miss.'

Charlotte, perched on a corner of the teacher's desk, smiled. Ms Weeks was looking right through her.

Marked absent, she didn't go into assembly. Instead she reclined on two giant beanbags and had a snooze. When the class returned, she sat in her usual place and trod on Toby Coughlin's foot under the table.

Toby winced and glared at Teresa Walsh. 'Give up, you spasmo!'

'What?' Teresa was indignant. 'I didn't *do* anything, you leper. *Ouch!* Miss, *tell* him, miss, he stamped on my foot for nothing. Oh, miss, it kills.'

'Toby Coughlin . . .?'

'I *didn't*, miss, it was her who stamped on *mine*. Oh, oh, I'm *crippled* miss, honest.'

'All right, that'll do,' rapped the teacher, 'from *both* of you.'

When everybody was busy Charlotte got up, crept to the board and scrawled a rude word in large letters. She returned to the beanbags and waited. After a minute Cecilia White noticed. Her gasp made everybody look up.

'Oh, miss, look on the board. It says . . .'

'I *know* what it says, Cecilia White, thank you very much.' Blushing furiously, the teacher strode to the board and rubbed out the word. 'Who wrote that? Was it *you*, Kevin Regan?'

'No way, miss.' The boy grinned. 'I didn't know you spelled it like that, miss.'

Charlotte chuckled, the sound masked by general laughter. Who said school was a drag? It was going to be a wonderful day.

CHAPTER
41

It all started to go wrong at half past eleven. By then Charlotte had done a few things, like giving Kylie Reid's hair a sharp tug during Silent Reading, tripping Esau Enright in P.E. so that instead of sailing over the vaulting horse he performed a spectacular sliding dive *under* it, and transferring the terrapin from its tank into Ms Weekes' coffee cup. The kids were enjoying an unusual morning and the teacher was starting to look a bit wild-eyed when there was a shy knock on the classroom door and Split le Beau walked in.

Charlotte couldn't believe it at first. She goggled. *Split le Beau, lead singer with Dead*

Ringer? It certainly *looked* like him, but why the heck would...? *Ah!* She recalled a rumour she'd heard, that Split's real name was Douglas Murgatroyd and that he'd once been a pupil at Holy Family.

'Douglas!' Ms Weekes stood up, smiling, as the world-famous superstar approached her desk. 'To what do we owe *this* honour?' A buzz of excitement rippled through the class, especially among the girls, most of whom had Dead Ringer posters on their bedroom walls.

The lad grinned. 'I was in the area, miss, so I thought I'd drop in. Hope I'm not wrecking your lesson?'

'No, no.' Her old pupil was making her blush harder than Charlotte's rude word had. 'It's lovely to see you, Douglas. Or should I be calling you Split?'

The lad shook his blond head. 'Oh no, miss – that's just for the fans.'

'I suspect you've got a few fans among these children, Douglas. Just look at their faces.'

Split grinned at the gobsmacked class. 'How you doing?' Sighs and moans rose from the young people. His grin broadened. 'How about

I sign some jotters or something?' He glanced at the teacher. 'That all right, miss?'

'Of course.' She smiled. 'I fancy I'd have a riot on my hands if I said no.'

In a flash, everybody had their jotters out and were scraping back their chairs.

Ms Weekes held up a hand. 'Just a minute!' Reluctantly they subsided. 'We'll do this properly, a table at a time.' She looked at the superstar. 'Why don't you sit at my desk, and we'll form a queue?' She stared at the class. 'An *orderly* queue.'

And so it was that over the next twenty minutes, every kid in the class got to chat briefly with the scrummy Split le Beau and collect a personalized autograph. Every kid in the class *except* Charlotte Webb, who had to hover at the back of the room, drooling.

He departed at five to twelve with a grin and a wave, having turned down the teacher's invitation to stay for a school dinner. The class, twitchy with residual adrenalin, tidied up under Ms Weekes' eagle eye and filed out to lunch. The teacher remained for a moment, gazing at the signature on her own jotter, then swept off towards the staffroom, leaving Charlotte cold, distraught and alone.

She crept unseen out of school and down the road. *Oh, Split – why today, of all days?* There was a spiteful wind, and it would be at least four hours before she could retrieve her clothes. She pulled a face. *Invisibility? You can keep it.*

CHAPTER
42

It stayed dry, so the barbie went ahead as scheduled. While Rosie was at school the two Bears built the oven out of stones borrowed from a nearby crumbling wall, then combed the woods for kindling and sawed up a fallen tree, stacking the logs beside the oven. In the afternoon they drove into Inchlake and loaded up the ambulance with sausages, steaks, fish, rolls and fizzy drinks. They bought firelighters too, just in case. When Rosie got home everything was ready.

'Looks great, Dad, Mum. The kids're going to love it.'

Mummy Bear smiled. 'What time did you tell them, sweetheart?'

'I said around seven. That OK?'

'Sure. Change into jeans and jumper, then help me carry chairs out. There'll be seven of us, is that right?'

'There's supposed to be, but I'm not sure about Conrad. He fell last night and knocked himself unconscious. They kept him in hospital overnight so he wasn't at school today.

'Oh, dear. What was he doing to fall, Rosie?'

'Messing about up Inchlake Ring with Carrie. She thinks he'll come if his mum and dad'll let him.'

'I don't think *I*'d let him come, sweetheart. Concussion's a funny thing.'

'I bet *he*'s not laughing.'

'You know what I mean.'

At five to seven the Waugh family Volvo appeared. Carrie got out, then to Rosie's delight Con emerged with a bandage round his head.

Daddy Bear bent by the driver's window. 'We'll keep an eye on the lad, Mr Waugh.' He smiled. 'Unless you want to stay, of course. You'd be very welcome.'

The twins' father shook his head. 'Thanks, but

my wife's got a job for me. I'll collect them around ten if that's all right.'

'Certainly is. See you then.' He gazed after the car as it crunched away down the bit of broken road.

It was five past seven and the kindling was ablaze when Peter arrived on foot. 'Hey, you'll never guess who *I* just saw.'

Rosie looked at him. 'Who?'

'Split le Beau.'

'Did you heck.'

'I *did*. He drove right past me in this fantastic Merc.'

Conrad shook his bandaged head. 'What would Split le Beau be doing in a dead hole like Inchlake, you moron? It was someone who *looked* like him, that's all.'

'No it was *him*, as close to me as you are now. He looked just like his poster.'

Carrie pulled a face. 'It's dark, Pete. You could've been mistaken.'

'He's not,' said Charlotte flatly. She'd arrived unnoticed by her friends, though Daddy Bear had seen her.

'How do *you* know?' asked Carrie. 'Did he

pass *you* in this fantastic Merc as well?'

'No, he came to school.'

'Yeah, right.'

'No, he *did*. He used to go there, that's why. Miss Weekes was his teacher.' She could see they didn't believe her. 'He signed everyone's jotter, so there.'

Conrad looked at her. 'Show us, then.'

'He didn't do mine.'

'Aaah, *see*.' He looked at the others. 'She's giving us a load of old cobblers.'

'No I'm *not*. I couldn't get mine done because nobody knew I was there. I was flipping *invisible*, see?'

'You went to school invisible?' Carrie chuckled. 'Wish *I'*d thought of that.'

'Well *I* wish I hadn't.'

Conrad nodded, fingering his bandage. 'Know what you mean, Spider. Not always fun, eh?'

'Hey, you kids!' Daddy Bear called from beyond the flames. 'Anyone ready for a sausage?'

Everybody was.

CHAPTER
43

'They were clever, those neolithic people,' said Daddy Bear. 'They knew hundreds of things we don't – things that are lost now. Forgotten. But they couldn't understand why invisibility didn't work any more once they reached the age of twelve or thirteen. It could have been useful to them in all sorts of ways. Hunting. Avoiding enemies. They kept walking widdershins round fairy rings but it never worked. They thought maybe they needed a *bigger* circle 'cause they were bigger, so they built stone circles like Inchlake Ring but that didn't work. They tried other shapes, such as spirals and swastikas and mazes. They carved 'em on rocks, cut 'em into the turf and built 'em out of stones but it was all no use. They never cracked it because it can't be done, but they left all these elaborate experiments behind and that's where some of our most famous patterns were copied from. It's why we have mazes. You know, those puzzles in comics where there's a tangle of lines and you've got to find your way to the centre without crossing one?'

'Wow!' Conrad swigged Coke from the bottle. 'I never knew *they* had anything to do with the Stone Age.'

Daddy Bear chuckled. 'Oh, you'd be amazed how much we owe to those guys, Con. Their forest clearance and farming formed a lot of our landscape. The countryside wouldn't look the way it does if they'd never lived.' He smiled round the circle of tired faces. 'They were here and then they were gone, and we must go too.'

There were mumbled protests as the big traveller clambered to his feet. 'Aw – can't we just have five more minutes, Daddy Bear? Three then? One? Fifteen seconds?'

He shook his head. 'Everything comes to an end, kids. Even the good stuff. Mr Waugh will be along any minute, and then Mummy Bear'll

drive Charlotte and Peter home while Rosie and
I clear up here.' He grinned. 'Hands up if you've
had a rotten time.'

There were no hands.

CHAPTER

44

Nothing much happened for a few days after the barbie. Saturday they all slept late. Sunday they discussed what they should do about Kippax and decided gloomily that there wasn't much they *could* do without proof. Conrad's bandage came off on Tuesday. Thursday night Charlotte brought Teresa Walsh's jotter to prove Split le Beau *had* visited his old school, and then it was Friday. Friday's always the best day at school, but this one was going to be really special.

While the children were at lunch a blue van came nosing into the yard. On its side in white letters were the words ROBERT KIPPAX – JOINERY &

GENERAL PROPERTY REPAIRS. Kippax senior was an old pupil of Inchlake School, and the van called about once a month to drop off a sack or two of nogs and offcuts the children could use in Design and Technology. When he saw the vehicle arrive, Mr Beecroft strode into the dining area and chose four volunteers to carry the wood into the DT store. One of these volunteers was Rosie.

The driver was sliding sacks out of the back of the van and dumping them on the tarmac. Rosie was relieved to see it wasn't Kippax himself, but one of his workers.

'Right.' The Bee organized his posse. 'Two to a sack. Four sacks. That's two journeys each. *Don't* try to carry one by yourself – there are no Arnold Schwarzeneggers at Inchlake School.' The volunteers tittered dutifully. The Bee smiled at the driver. 'Thanks. And thank Mr Kippax for me, will you?'

'I will. Tarra.' The man swung himself into the cab and drove off, anxious to be clear of the yard before the kids came swarming out.

Rosie's partner was Carl Foxcroft. She'd tried to team up with the other girl, but The Bee had suggested girl-boy pairs and he was the boss.

Carl smiled nastily as they lugged their burden through a side door. 'You wanna take this lot home, gipsy. Make a lot of clothes-pegs, this would.'

'We don't do pegs, you moron, and we're not gipsies.' She eyeballed him. '*You* could use it though – fill that empty space between your ears.'

As they dumped the heavy sack on the floor it collapsed sideways, spilling a few nogs. Rosie squatted and scooped them up. As she went to tip them back in the bag, she saw a strip of gold-painted wood sticking out. It was pretty, with a pattern of curly leaves glistening along its length. She pulled it out. It was about a metre long. At either end was a short, ungilded section cut at an angle. It reminded her of . . .

'What is it?' Carl Foxcroft peered at the strip.

Rosie shrugged, though her heart was racing. 'Dunno. Nice though, isn't it? Think I'll have it.' She straightened up.

The boy leered. 'I'll get you done.'

Rosie stared at him. 'You've got a short memory, Foxy. Remember that day on the field?'

'What day? What you on about, gipsy?'

'Oh come *on* – you remember. Clothes, *walking by themselves*?'

'Oh . . . yeah.' He looked uncomfortable, as though he'd been reminded of something he'd rather forget. 'What about it?'

'*This* about it, moron.' She thrust her face into his. 'That stuff's nothing – absolutely *nothing*, compared to what'll happen if you grass me up to The Bee. You got that?'

'Uh . . . yeah. Yeah, OK.'

'It *better* be OK.' She hid the gilded strip in a corner, right at the back of the store where it was dark. She leaned it against the wall behind a stack of cardboard boxes. The place wasn't kept locked. She could slip back later and get it.

She smiled to herself, going back for the second load. *I could be wrong I suppose, but I think that strip's what we've been waiting for. I think we've got our proof.*

CHAPTER
45

Bob Kippax was agitated. He kept coming outside, glancing around and going back in the Portakabin which served as his office. After a bit he called across the yard to a young man in overalls who was stacking new timber. 'Where's Leonard gone with the van, Malcolm?'

The young man slid a board onto the stack and turned. 'It's the first of the month, Mr Kippax. He's down the school with the offcuts.'

'Ah, right. Where did he take 'em from, d'you know?'

'Well – all over, I suppose, same as usual. I mean, this delivery had just come in so I wasn't taking much notice. Why?'

Kippax ignored the question, gesturing towards a dilapidated shed. 'Did he take anything out of there?'

'He might have. Like I say, I wasn't watching him. I was busy.'

'OK.'

He was halfway up the office steps when he heard a motor. The van swung into the yard. He waited while the driver parked and got out. 'Leonard?'

'Yes, boss?'

'The stuff for the school. Did you get any of it from the shed?'

'A few bits, yeah.'

'Any *old* stuff?'

'Don't remember, could've been. Why – is something up?'

'The frames from those flipping pictures're in the shed, only there's a piece missing. You've not taken *that* to the school, have you?'

Leonard shook his head. 'Don't think so, boss, but I couldn't swear to it.'

'You couldn't *swear* to it?' Kippax glared at the hapless driver. 'You know what'll happen if you have and somebody spots it, don't you?'

'Sure, boss, big trouble. Want me to go back there and check?'

'Oh yeah. What you gonna say? *Excuse me Mr Beecroft, d'you think I could take a look at those off-cuts I brought just now – I might have put stolen property in by mistake?* No.' He continued up the steps. 'You've screwed up enough for one day, Leonard. Get back to your work. I'll sort it.' He went in the office and picked up the phone.

CHAPTER
46

First period after lunch one of the little kids knocked on the classroom door and came in. 'Please, miss, can Lee Kippax go to the office? He's wanted on the phone.'

Miss Blackburn sighed. 'Yes, all right. Off you go, Lee, but don't be all afternoon.'

'Hello?' The school secretary had left the office to give him privacy.

'That you, Lee?'

'Dad. What's up?'

'Listen. Do you know where they keep the wood?'

'What wood?'

'The wood I send round for CDT or whatever they call it nowadays.'

'Oh, yeah. The DT store. It's sort of round the side of the . . .'

'I don't want to know how to *find* it, you dummy. Can you get in there?'

'Well yeah, but . . .'

'It's not locked?'

'No.'

'Right. Get yourself round there, *now*. Leonard's just dropped a load off. Four bags. I want you to search 'em. You're looking for a piece of picture frame, gilded, about a metre long. You got that?'

'Yes, Dad, but I can't go now. We're in the middle of Geography.'

'I don't care if you're in the middle of the Pacific Ocean, you cretin. Get round there and find that wood, unless you want to be visiting me in jail.'

The prospect of seeing his father locked up for a year or two appealed to the boy, but he was a dutiful son. 'I . . . I'll do my best, Dad. Tarra.' He hung up.

I can't go now. *Old Blackbum'd come looking for me. She'd think I was either dodging her lesson or nicking from the store. Both, probably. I'll go at half three.*

'Finished?' asked the secretary as Lee emerged.

'Oh – yes, miss. Thanks.'

'Not trouble at home, I hope?'

'No, miss.' He returned to the classroom. *Dad's trouble is, he panics. Never get anywhere if you panic.* He picked up his pencil, made a dot in the middle of the Pacific Ocean and smiled.

Me.

CHAPTER
47

Half past three. The moment Miss Blackburn dismissed the class, Rosie headed for the DT store. She'd just slipped inside and pulled the door to behind her when it opened again to admit Lee Kippax. He scowled at her.

'What's your game, gipsy?'

Rosie looked at him. 'What's yours?'

'The Bee sent me to tidy up in here.'

'Oh. Well, I was just looking for something.'

'What?'

'Doesn't matter, it's not here. See you.' She slipped past him.

Blast! Now what do I do? She went out into the yard. *The Bee never sent him, he's after that bit of* wood. *That's why he was wanted on the phone. Our bit of proof's about to disappear.*

She glanced around, hoping to spot Peter or the twins among the departing pupils but it seemed they'd already gone. All she could think to do was hide behind the bike shed and watch the door till Lee came out. Maybe he wouldn't find what he was looking for.

He didn't. At a quarter to four he emerged empty handed, looking glum. Rosie's heart soared. *You can't hide a metre of wood in your pocket, but I can't* believe *he missed it.* She watched as the boy trailed disconsolately out of the yard, then slipped back inside.

It was there, in the corner where she'd propped it. She grabbed it, peeked round the door to make sure no cleaner was about and left the building, intent on catching up with Peter and the twins. She was in such a hurry that she jogged right past the phone box without noticing that Lee was inside, and that he'd clocked her.

CHAPTER
48

As Rosie approached the phone box, Kippax senior was blasting his son's eardrum. 'OF *COURSE* SHE WAS LOOKING FOR THE SAME THING AS YOU, YOU DAFT LITTLE GROMMIT. SHE'S PROBABLY IN THERE RIGHT NOW SHOVING IT IN HER . . .'

'Dad!' The boy goggled through the glass. 'You're *right*, she's just gone past with it in her hand.'

'WELL WHAT YOU *WAITING* FOR, YOU PILLOCK? GET *AFTER* HER – GET IT OFF HER. GO *ON*!'

'OK, Dad. I'm off.' Lee slammed down the handset and burst from the kiosk. Rosie was disappearing round a curve, pumping the bit of frame up and down like a relay runner with the baton. He raced after her.

At first he did well because the girl didn't know she was being chased. She jogged up the road, swerving through kids dawdling home-ward, expecting any minute to see Peter and the twins in front of her. Lee, going full pelt, was closing the gap. Then, when he was no more than twenty metres behind, some daft kid swerved into his path and they collided. 'Hey!' cried the startled child. 'Why the *heck* can't you watch where you're going?' Normally Lee would have taken time out to flatten him, but Rosie had heard the kid's cry and glanced back. As soon as she saw Lee she knew what he was after and put on a spurt. Raised in the country, she could run like a hare. In seconds the gap had widened to thirty metres, then forty, then fifty. The thought of what his dad would do to him if he let the gipsy get away acted as an accelerator to Lee, who pounded after her.

Rosie was lean and fit but Lee was desperate and she couldn't shake him off. She was blow-ing hard and getting a stitch in her side when she saw Peter and the twins ahead.

'Hey, wait!' They recognized her voice and turned. Rosie lolloped up to them, gasping. 'This.' She held out the gilded wood. 'Proof, I think. Off up the Manor . . . make sure. Grab *him.*' She jerked her head towards Lee, who had spotted her in company and slowed. 'Give me a start, OK?' She staggered on.

Lee swerved into the middle of the road to avoid them. They spread out to block him and he ran roaring at Carrie, thinking she'd chicken out. She didn't. As he charged her she lowered her head and rammed him in the pit of his stomach. He collapsed onto his knees, hugging his middle while his face turned purple. As he toppled sideways the two boys threw themselves on him, pinning him to the ground. Carrie glanced up the road. Rosie was well clear but limping. They'd need to hold Lee for a minute or two but it wasn't a problem. Badly winded, the bully lay spreadeagled like a dead starfish under Con and Pete. She'd just permitted herself a faint smile when she heard the sound of a motor moving at speed. A blue van came zooming up the road and screeched to a halt. The driver's door was flung open. Bob Kippax emerged looking murderous. He strode towards them.

CHAPTER
49

'GERROFFIM! LERRIMUP!' The two startled boys rolled off their victim as his father stormed towards them. Lee sat up, wrapped his arms round his stomach and rocked. Kippax glared down at him without sympathy. 'Where's that bit of wood, you useless lump – don't tell me you didn't *get* it?'

'I . . . she ran off, Dad.'

'She's a GIRL, you plonker. Girls don't *run*, they flap about. Which way's she gone – where does she *live*, for Pete's sake?'

'She's not gone home,' blurted Peter. 'She's . . .'

'SHUT IT, PETE!' This from Carrie.

Peter clapped a hand to his mouth. 'S . . . sorry.'

Kippax eyeballed him. 'Where *has* she gone, boy? Spit it out or I'll shove two fingers up your nose and pull an eyeball down.'

'I . . . I dunno, Mr Kippax.'

'Yes you do. I bet it's the *police station*, isn't it?'

'No.'

'Good.' The man smiled tightly. 'So what does *that* leave?' He frowned, thinking.

Peter and the twins started backing away, ready to run. Lee had risen to his knees and was knocking dust off his uniform. He gave his father a sulky look. 'Bet *I* know where she's off to.'

Kippax senior glanced at his son. 'Come on then, Einstein – enlighten us.'

'What – in front of *them*?' Lee nodded towards the three children.

Kippax glared at them. 'Make yourselves scarce NOW, or I'll report you for assault. GO ON!' He watched as they pelted up the road, then turned to his son. 'OK – where? And *do* get up out of the dirt, you boneless twit.'

Lee clambered to his feet. 'That bit of frame – it's off a painting, isn't it? One of those nicked from the manor.'

''*Course* it is. Why else would I care if someone got hold of it? Where's she *gone* with it?'

'Up the Manor.'

'The *Manor*? What the heck *for*?'

'To make sure.'

'Make sure of *what*, you prawn?'

'To make sure it *is* off one of the Turners. She'll show old Miss whatsername – Massingberd – then take it to the police.'

The man's eyes narrowed. 'D'you think so? D'you think she's that smart – a ruddy *gipsy*?'

'She's not a gipsy, and she *is* pretty smart. I'd bet a year's pocket money that's where she's gone.'

Kippax chuckled unpleasantly. 'You just *did*, sunshine. Come on.' He strode towards the van.

CHAPTER
50

They ran till Lee, his father and the van were way behind. When they stopped, panting and swiping sweat from their foreheads, Conrad gasped, 'D'you reckon Lee *does* know where Rosie's gone?'

Peter shrugged. 'Dunno. His dad called him Einstein, but Frankenstein's more like it. *I* don't see how he could know.'

Carrie pulled a face. 'He might *guess* though, and I wouldn't want to be Rosie if he does. I think we'd better get up there in case she needs help.'

Peter looked at her. 'How could *we* help, Carrie? You saw what old Kippax is like when he's mad. We need the police.'

Carrie sighed. 'Yes, Pete, I *know* we need the police, but the police need evidence and *we* haven't got it – *Rosie* has. We're *kids* – they wouldn't believe a word we said.'

'So *you* suggest something.'

'OK.' She gazed at the two boys. 'I know we can't stand up to Kippax as we are *now*, but it'd be different if we were invisible, right?'

'Ugh!' Conrad shivered. 'No more invisible for *me*, Sis. Not after what happened to me last time.'

'You were being a div last time, Con. Messing about. There'd be none of that this time.' She turned to Peter. 'Tell him, Pete.'

Peter pouted. 'Actually I'm not keen myself, Carrie. Stuff can happen when you're invisible. Bad stuff. I vote we tell a grown-up – our parents or The Bee or somebody.'

Carrie snorted. 'Waste of time, Pete. Nobody'd *believe* us. Listen – we're supposed to be a gang, aren't we? Well – *aren't* we?'

'Yeah.'

'I suppose.'

'And the point about gangs is that members stick together, right? Help one another.'

'Uh . . . yeah.'

'Hmmm . . .'

'Well then – *Rosie*'s a member, she could be in trouble – in *danger* – so it's up to us to help her. Am I right?'

'Haaar.'

'Umph.'

'Is that a *yes*, or what?'

'Ah . . . yeah.'

'Uh . . . mmm.'

'Well come *on* then – let's go.'

'Where?'

'The *ice house*, of course. How *else* do we go invisible? Move.'

'Just when I'm *dying* for my flipping tea,' groaned Conrad.

CHAPTER
51

Charlotte dawdled along the road feeling glum. *OK, so it's Friday. No school tomorrow, but it's also the first weekiversary of not getting Split le Beau's autograph, so it's a bummer. Everything's a bummer, and invisibility's the biggest bummer of them all.* She aimed a kick at a drift of fallen leaves, turned the corner and stopped dead. Right in front of her, not twenty metres away, stood a long silver Mercedes. Beside it, leaning on its gleaming roof, smoking a cigarette, was Split le Beau.

She couldn't believe it at first, but stood gaping as her jaw dropped and her knees turned to jelly. *It isn't him. It can't be. He's a superstar. He wouldn't hang around this dead hole for a week.* She was gathering her courage to go up to him and say, *Excuse me, but has anybody ever told you you look just like Split le Beau?* when he noticed her and smiled across the polished roof.

'Hello.'

'Huuu . . . uuu . . . hello. Is it *you*, really?'

'It's me, really.' The cigarette wagged as he spoke. 'What's *your* name?'

'Charlotte. Charlotte Webb. I . . .' She'd been about to say *I saw you at school*, but changed it to 'I missed you at school. Last week. I was away.'

He grinned round the cigarette. 'Shame. Still you've caught me now, haven't you?'

'Uh . . . yes.' She giggled, feeling her cheeks flame. 'Can I . . . would you mind . . . ?' Fumbling with her bag.

'An autograph?' He smiled. 'Don't worry about paper, I've got some snapshots somewhere.' He opened the driver's door and stooped to the map pocket. Here y'are.' He rested the photo on the roof and spoke the words he was inscribing as Charlotte moved closer. 'To Charlotte – sincerely – Split.' He looked up. 'What's today's date?' She told him in a hoarse whisper and he added it with a flourish. 'There. That all right for you,

Charlotte?' He handed her the glossy photo.

She glanced at it, nodding. 'It's . . . fabulous, Split. Fabulous.'

The superstar chuckled. 'Good. Well – better get on. Got an appointment at four. 'Bye, Charlotte.'

'Oh, yes. Bye, Spl . . .'

He was swinging himself into the driver's seat when there was a sound of running footsteps and Rosie came tearing round the corner. She saw the car, then Charlotte, and as he leaned across to get the door, she saw Split le Beau. 'Wha . . .?' The shock broke her rhythm. She came to a panting halt, looking from Charlotte to Split and back to Charlotte. 'Charlotte, how the . . . what're *you* doing with . . . oh, heck!' She glanced behind, held up the bit of frame. 'Gotta go. The Manor. Kippax behind. I'll phone later. See you.' With a last yearning glance in Split's direction she ran on, sweat glistening on her forehead.

His chuckle diverted Charlotte's attention from her friend's flight. 'What was all *that* about?'

'Oh . . .' She shook her head. 'It's nothing. That's Rosie. We're just . . .' She broke off as a blue van came screeching round the corner. Split had to slam his door to keep it from being torn off its hinges as the vehicle swerved by. He shook his head. 'Crazy folk you got around here, Charlotte. You better . . .'

'*Please*, Split . . .?'

He looked up at her. 'What *is* it kid? What's going on?'

'I'm not sure, but I think that van's after Rosie. D'you think you could . . .?' *Never get in some-one's car*, hissed her mind, but surely . . . Split le Beau . . .

'Sure, hop in.' He leaned across, opened the passenger door. 'Did I hear your friend mention the Manor?'

'Yeah, that's where she's gone I think.'

'Weird.' He put the car in gear and it shot forward, slamming Charlotte back in her seat.

She looked across at him. 'What?'

'The Manor. It's where my four o'clock appointment is. Hold on.' They screamed round a bend and sped on.

Charlotte felt unreal.

CHAPTER
52

Made it, and still no sign of Kippax. Rosie hurried up the driveway and mounted the mossy steps. The yellow Polo was parked at the bottom, which meant the nurse was here again. Rosie hoped she wouldn't stop her seeing Miss Massingberd.

There was a bell-push screwed to the door. She thumbed it, glancing over her should. *Come on, Flo Nightingale – it's urgent.* She knew it would be the nurse and not Miss Massingberd who came to the door. It felt like ages before she heard footsteps. The door opened a crack and the nurse frowned down at her.

'Yes?'

'Can I see Miss Massingberd for a minute, please? It's *really* important.'

'Oh it *is*, is it? Why?'

'It's about her pictures. The ones that were pinched. I know who did it.'

'*Do* you, now?'

'Yes, look.' Rosie held out the piece of frame. 'I think this is off one of them. If Miss Massingberd could just . . .'

'I'm sorry. Miss Massingberd is unwell, and besides she's expecting somebody at any minute. If you come back tomorrow . . .'

'It'll be too late.' She heard an engine down by the road, knew it was Kippax. 'Here.' She thrust the gilded strip at the woman. 'Take this to the old lady. She'll recognize it.'

She was halfway down the steps when the nurse called after her. 'What's your *name*, little girl?'

'Rosie.' She flung the word over her shoulder without stopping. 'Rosie Walk.' She could see the van through thin autumn foliage. Another second and the driver would see *her*. She heard the door close behind her as she raced for the shrubbery.

Too late. She was less than halfway there

when the van overtook her, slewing to a stop in a spray of gravel. The driver's door flew open and Kippax baled out. Before she had time to cry out or change direction he'd grabbed her. A brawny arm circled her neck, a rough palm clamped her mouth.

'OK, gipsy, where is it?'

'What?' She kicked and writhed and tried to bite his hand.

'You know what. *Come on – what you done with it?*' The arm round her neck tightened. She began to choke. Through her tears she could see Lee in the passenger seat, watching. The pressure eased a fraction and she croaked, 'I don't know what you mean.' She prayed the nurse was showing the strip to Miss Massingberd right now.

'YOU KNOW ALL RIGHT.' He was shouting, shaking her. 'SPIT IT OUT OR I'LL THROTTLE THE LIFE OUT OF YOU!'

She was choking. Flashes in her eyes like stars exploding and blackness round the edges, flooding in. A hand gripped her flailing forearm. A hand she couldn't see. A *third* hand, and a voice hissed in her ear, *The ice house. Say it's in the ice house. Carrie*'s voice.

She battered the brawny arm with both fists. The stranglehold loosened. 'Well?'

'The ice house. I hid it in the ice house.'

'That's better.' The arm was removed. Rosie sucked in air as the man grabbed a fistful of hair to steer her by. The blackness was receding. 'Come on – show me.'

She was stumbling through a tangle of neglected shrubs, her head thrust forward. Twigs scraped her face and Kippax kept treading on her heels as they waded through wet leaves. He was panting with exertion as he shoved her along, sounding like a big dog. The ice house came in sight through the trees. What would she do when they reached it? What would *Kippax* do to her when he realized she'd lied?

Hey, Rosie, stay cool. Carrie whispered to you, right? That means the Invisibles're here. Or does it? What if being strangled makes you hear things that aren't really there?

Well if that's *the explanation you'll be hearing 'em again, dude. Real soon.*

CHAPTER
53

The nurse punched in the number, heard the first ring and handed the receiver to the old lady. Miss Massingberd held it to her ear, gazing at the strip of gilded wood on the table. Somebody picked up.

'Hello? Is this the police? Good afternoon, Constable Stables. This is Miss Massingberd, calling from the Manor. That's right, the Manor. There's been a . . . development, I suppose you'd say, in the matter of my stolen paintings. Well, a child rang my bell a few minutes ago, claiming to know who took the paintings. A child, yes. A little girl. She handed my nurse part of a picture frame and it *is* from one of my Turners. Her name?' Miss Massingberd shot the nurse an enquiring glance and lip-read the woman's response. 'Walk, apparently. Rosie Walk. Oh, you *know* about her? *Is* she a gipsy? I really couldn't say, Constable – didn't see her myself. Oh, I don't think ... she'd hardly come up here and ring the bell if she was the thief, would she? Her *father*? But why would a daughter ... did you say *double bluff*? I'm afraid I'm not familiar with the term. Oh, I don't think she's here *now*, Constable. The nurse told me she ran off. Come by all means if you think that's best. You can collect the bit of frame if nothing else. Good, then I'll see you presently. Goodbye.'

The nurse put down the receiver. 'On their way, eh?'

The old lady nodded. 'Keen, our Constable Stables. Very. Doesn't like gipsies by the sound of him.' She looked at the nurse. 'Did the child look like a criminal to *you*, my dear?'

The nurse pulled a face. 'No, but then if criminals *looked* like criminals there'd be no need for detectives, would there?'

CHAPTER
54

Rosie knuckled her eyes and sniffled. No fun, being lowered into darkness by your hair. It hurts, plus she was dead scared. Who wouldn't be, alone in an abandoned ice house with a guy like Kippax? Even down here he didn't relax his grip. Her scalp felt tender, as though it was lifting from her skull. He squeezed and she cried out, the sound echoing eerily in the damp blackness.

'Right, gipsy . . . where is it?'

'This way.' She chose a direction at random, creeping forward. *Where are you, Carrie? Do something for goodness' sake*, quick. *Don't let me die down here.*

They must have been halfway across the floor when Kippax gasped and swiped at something in the blackness. The movement caused a tug on Rosie's hair and she yelped.

'What *is* it?'

'Dunno.' The man peered into the gloom. 'Bat, maybe. Never mind.' He shoved her forward, but they'd taken only two paces when there was a sharp scraping noise and a match flared. Kippax started violently. 'WHO'S THERE?' The flame steadied, trembling in a draught. He couldn't see the hand that held it. 'WHO IS IT?'

'Nobody, Robert Kippax. Nobody at all.' Rosie's heart soared. The voice was distorted by echo and disguised to sound like a ghost's, but she recognized it and smiled. Good old Pete.

Kippax was shaken. Rosie felt the hand that held her hair start to twitch and bit her lip to keep from giggling. The match dwindled and died. The man continued to stare at the place, seeing a greenish blob. 'I'M WARNING YOU, WHOEVER YOU ARE,' he bellowed. 'NOBODY MESSES WITH BOB KIPPAX. *NOBODY.*'

'That's *right*, Robert Kippax, and that's exactly who *I* am. Nobody. Look.' A second match, in a different spot. This one moved up and down, from side to side, back and forth, its little globe of brightness revealing no part of the speaker. The tremor in Kippax's hand grew more pronounced. *Any second now*, thought Rosie, *he's gonna forget I'm here and let go.* For the moment though he went on deploying the bully's weapon, bluster.

'YOU'LL PAY FOR THIS. YOU CAN'T STAY IN HERE FOR EVER AND WHEN YOU COME OUT I'LL BE WAITING.' He stared into the blackness, breathing heavily. Rosie stood absolutely still, saying nothing.

'You are *so* wrong, Robert Kippax. *So* wrong. We *can* stay here for ever, for this is our hoo – ooom.' Rosie nearly burst out laughing as Carrie made the word *home* sound like the hoot of an owl. Its echo had scarcely faded when the voice continued. 'You have entered our home un-invited, and for that you must be punished.' At this point somebody evidently struck the man because he swung round with an oath and threw a punch, relinquishing his hold on Rosie's hair to do so. She stepped lightly to one side and was lost to him at once.

'HEY!' The frightened bully spun round, groping for his victim. Three metres away Rosie stood holding her breath, knowing she was as safe from him now as if she were on Mars. 'DON'T THINK I CAN'T SEE YOU, GIPSY, 'CAUSE I CAN. GET HERE – *NOW*!'

'Temper, Robert Kippax.' Con's voice, hollow in the gloom.

Kippax turned slowly on the spot, unable to tell where the speaker was. 'YOU DON'T SCARE ME WITH YOUR SILLY PUT-ON VOICE, SO DON'T THINK IT.'

'You *sound* afraid, notwithstanding, and I see you've lost your prisoner. Perhaps you should leave.'

'I'M NOT LEAVING TILL I GET WHAT I CAME FOR.'

'You'll get what you came for if you *stay*, Robert Kippax – that I promise you.'

'HOWDYA MEAN?'

'Stay, and find out.'

'I'm not. I'm going, but I'll be waiting, and when you come out I'll make you wish you'd never been born.' He moved towards a faint luminescence which marked the position of the entrance. 'THAT GOES FOR YOU TOO, GIPSY.'

It was then the laughter started. Demoniacal laughter from every direction at once, echoing and re-echoing till it seemed the ice house harboured a thousand devils. He *tried* to go slowly. *Tried* to hold on to what was left of his dignity, but the laughter woke a memory from the distant past – a film he'd seen as a kid, set in a creepy Victorian asylum. He hadn't slept properly for weeks after watching that film, and he'd nursed a secret dread ever since – a dread of losing his mind and being dragged off screaming to a place like the asylum in that film. He quickened his pace, muttering to himself as the laughter ricocheted inside his skull. *I'm not mad, just because I see matches that strike themselves and hover in the air, like . . . like Lee with that ball. (Runs in families, madness.) I'm not mad. Not mad.* He stumbled sobbing towards the light and looked up and there, gazing down at him, was the most famous pop star in England.

Of course he was.

CHAPTER
55

Split's Mercedes had swung through the gateposts of Inchlake Manor seven minutes behind the blue van. It could have been two minutes and Kippax might never have got Rosie as far as the ice house, but Split missed the turn first time and had to backtrack. By the time he and Charlotte came in sight of the house there was no sign of either the joiner or the girl, but the van was there with its engine ticking over and Lee in the driver's seat. The boy's jaw dropped when Split stuck his head through the window.

'Rosie – where is she?'

'Uh – *you*. You're just like that singer – you know – Split le Beau?'

'I *am* Split, and I'll split *you* if you don't answer my question. WHERE'S ROSIE?'

'You're *him*? Wow! Uh . . . Rosie said the *ice house*, whatever that is. They went that way.' He flapped an arm towards the shrubbery.

'They?'

'Huh?'

'You said *they*.'

'Yeah – Rosie and Dad.'

The star straightened up and looked at Charlotte. 'The ice house?'

'Yes, I've been there.'

'Lead on then, *quick*.'

They heard the racket in the ice house long before they reached it. 'Oh God!' sobbed Charlotte, 'he's *murdering* her.' They pelted towards the mossy dome and round it, reaching the doorway in time to see a dishevelled Bob Kippax scrabbling to haul himself out. Peals of ghastly laughter pursued him as he heaved his top half clear and flopped gasping on the grass. Noticing a crocodile shoe three centimetres from his nose he looked up, straight into the face of Split le Beau.

'Aaaagh!' He writhed on the ground,

kneading his eyes with his fists. 'I'm *not* mad, I tell you. *Not* mad.'

As the ice house laughter dwindled, there was a crashing in the bushes and a policeman burst out yelling, 'I *know* you're in there, Miss Walk. Come out quietly and you won't get...' He skidded to a halt, goggling at the man on the ground. '*Bob?*'

'I'm *not* mad!' Kippax got up on his hands and knees and crawled towards the officer. 'They're *real*, those matches. I *saw* them strike themselves. Wave themselves about. And the voices, laughing at me. *They're* real too.' He grabbed his school chum's ankles and rested his forehead on the toecaps of his boots. 'Don't let them put me away, Steve. Prison, yeah – I *deserve* that, but not the ... not the *loony* bin.'

As Kippax blubbed on Stables' size elevens, there was movement inside the ice house and Rosie stuck her head out. 'Oh hi, Charlotte. Glad you could make it. Everyone else is here.' Three grinning faces appeared. Carrie recognized Split and squealed. '*Oooh*, look who it is. Shift yourself, Rosie – let me get *at* him.'

Split leaned towards Charlotte and whispered in her ear. 'Your friend seems to be OK so I'll slip away before I'm mobbed. Nice meeting you, Charlotte.'

As the superstar vanished into the bushes, Bob Kippax plucked at the constable's trousers.

'See – *he*'s real, isn't he, and you wouldn't expect to see . . .' He gestured to where he'd last seen Split, but he wasn't there. Stables glanced where Kippax was pointing, then down at his friend. '*Who*, Bob? Who wouldn't you expect to see?'

Kippax appealed to Charlotte. '*Tell* him, kid. Tell him Split le Beau was here.'

Charlotte frowned and shook her head. 'Split le Beau? *Here?* I'm afraid you're *seeing* things, Mr Kippax.'

CHAPTER
56

Hometime, Friday October 22nd. Three weeks had rolled by since the exciting events at Inchlake Manor. The weather had grown colder, especially first thing in the morning. Next week the clocks would go back. Winter was closing in.

'So, children.' Miss Blackburn stood up, rubbed her hands together and smiled. 'The time has come when we must all say goodbye to Rosie Walk.' She beamed at Rosie, who had become something of a heroine since her ordeal in the ice house. 'I don't suppose we'll ever see you again, Rosie, but I'm sure everybody here joins me in wishing you good luck in the future.' A murmur of assent rippled round the classroom. Every eye was on Rosie. She blushed.

'Thanks, miss. Thanks, everybody.' She smiled. 'I don't expect to miss Inchlake very much, because we travellers see so many places and after a while they all run into one. I never miss schools either, but I do miss *people*, and I know I'm going to miss all of you.'

The children, unsure what response was called for, smiled and nodded. Then somebody at the back started clapping. Everybody looked round. It was Lee Kippax, who'd become a different boy – a *happier* boy since his father went away. He looked at his classmates, growled 'Come *on* then,' and everybody began to clap, including the teacher. Rosie picked up her bag and hurried from the room with flaming cheeks.

'Good send-off or what?' grinned Peter, when they were clear of the school.

Rosie groaned. 'I nearly *died*. Trust old Lee to embarrass the heck out of me at the last minute.'

Conrad chuckled. 'He's *grateful* to you, Rosie. Life's really opened up for him since that awful dad of his went to prison.'

Rosie grinned. 'Not very nice for *him*, though.'

'Oh, I don't know,' said Carrie. 'He'll be

relieved it's prison and not the loony-bin after what he saw in that ice house.'

'*Thought* he saw,' amended Peter, straight-faced.

Carrie nodded. 'That's what I meant.'

'Boo!' They jumped and squealed as Charlotte sprang from behind the phone box.

Rosie goggled. 'How'd *you* get here so quick?'

Charlotte grinned. 'Told Miss Weekes I had a dentist appointment. Well – I couldn't let you go without saying goodbye, could I? Besides, I've got a secret to tell.'

Carrie looked at her. 'If you tell, it'll stop being a secret.'

'No it won't. It'll be a secret known only to our gang. I know you won't spread it around.'

'What is it, then?'

'It's about Miss Massingberd.'

'Miss *Massingberd*?' Conrad groaned. 'Can't be anything exciting then, can it?'

'Well – it's about Split le Beau as well.'

'Miss Massingberd and Split le Beau? Don't tell me . . . they're getting married, right?'

'No, you smeghead! Miss Massingberd's off to live with her sister in Devon, and guess who's buying the Manor?'

'Not . . . ?'

'Yes – Split le Beau. Isn't that great? We'll see him all the time.'

Rosie shook her head. '*I* won't.'

'Oh no, you *won't*, will you? I never thought of that.'

'Well don't let it worry you, Charlotte. I'm used to meeting people and then not seeing them any more.' She smiled. 'It's about to happen right now, in fact.' They'd reached the old Cleeston Road. Rosie stopped. 'Listen, you guys – long goodbyes screw me up, so it'd be cool if you didn't come any further with me, OK?' There was a break in her voice, as though she was talking round an aching lump. The others looked at their feet.

Peter murmured, 'I thought I'd come and say thanks to your folks, Rosie. Y'know – for the barbie and that.'

Rosie shook her head. 'No need, Pete. They know you enjoyed yourself.'

'Yeah, but . . .'

'It's not what people *say*, Pete – it's what they *do*. They only had to look at you to know the evening was a hit.'

He nodded. 'OK.'

'You off tonight?' asked Conrad.

Rosie shook her head. 'Tomorrow, first thing. We'll be at Warwick by lunchtime.' She looked at the four of them. 'Think you'll go invisible now and then?'

'Hmm.' They shuffled, looking down.

'Winter's coming on,' mumbled Conrad. 'Too cold. Next spring, maybe.'

Peter nodded. 'Yeah, spring.'

Carrie said nothing at all.

Rosie nodded, knowing they'd never be invisible again. Some things sound fun till you try them, then you discover the downside. 'I'm off, then. Think of me sometimes if you don't forget.'

Peter blinked and swallowed. ''*Course* we won't forget, how could we?' His smile was watery. 'The Inchlake Invisibles. We'll *always* be your gang, Rosie, even if we never meet again.'

Rosie smiled. 'Great last line, Pete. Look after one another. 'Bye.'

THE END

ABOUT THE AUTHOR

Robert Swindells left school at fifteen and worked as a copyholder on a local newspaper. At seventeen he joined the RAF for three years, two of which he served in Germany. He then worked as a clerk, an engineer and a printer before training and working as a teacher. He is now a full-time writer and lives on the Yorkshire moors.

He has written many books for young readers. *Room 13* won the 1990 Children's Book Award. *Abomination* won the 1999 Stockport Children's Book Award and was shortlisted for the Whitbread Prize, the Sheffield Children's Book Award, the Lancashire Children's Book Award *and* the 1999 Children's Book Award. His books for older readers include *Stone Cold*, which won the 1994 Carnegie Medal, as well as the award-winning *Brother in the Land*. As well as writing, Robert Swindells enjoys keeping fit, travelling and reading.

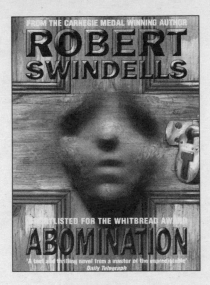

Martha is twelve, and very different from other kids. No TV.
No computer. No cool clothes. Especially, no *friends.*

It's all because of her parents. Strict members of a religious group,
their rules dominate Martha's life. But one rule is the most important
of all: Martha must never ever invite anyone home. If she does,
their terrible secret – Abomination – could be revealed . . .

'A taut and thrilling novel from a master of the unpredictable'
Daily Telegraph

**WINNER OF THE 1999 STOCKPORT
CHILDREN'S BOOK AWARD**

**WINNER OF THE 1999 SHEFFIELD
CHILDREN'S BOOK AWARD**

**SHORTLISTED FOR THE WHITBREAD PRIZE,
THE LANCASHIRE CHILDREN'S BOOK AWARD**
and **THE 1999 CHILDREN'S BOOK AWARD**

ISBN 0 440 86362 7

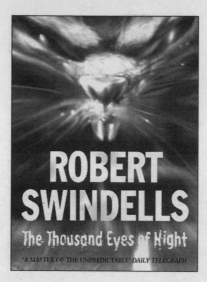

ROBERT SWINDELLS

The Thousand Eyes of Night

'A MASTER OF THE UNPREDICTABLE' *DAILY TELEGRAPH*

The skeleton lay on its back. The jaws gaped and one arm lay across the chest as though flung there to ward off a blow . . .

The Tangle is a long, narrow stretch of derelict land, a wilderness of weeds and rubbish with an old railway tunnel yawning blackly at one end. No-one – not even bullying Gary Deacon – dares venture far into its sooty darkness. But it is here that twelve-year-old Tan and his friends make a grisly discovery – a discovery that is to plunge them into a terrifying adventure as the tunnel slowly unfolds its sinister secret . . .

'A tremendous climax' *Growing Point*

ISBN 0 440 86316 3

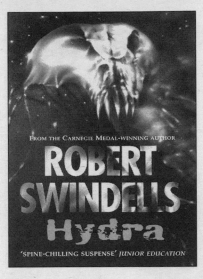

FROM THE CARNEGIE MEDAL-WINNING AUTHOR

ROBERT SWINDELLS

Hydra

'SPINE-CHILLING SUSPENSE' *JUNIOR EDUCATION*

*The floater moved out into the barn. Eyeless, it felt the faint
pull of starlight and followed, passing through the great
open doorway and drifting away in the dark . . .*

Friends Ben and Midge are determined to investigate when
mysterious corn circles begin to appear in the fields around
Cansfield Farm. But when they sneak out at night to explore,
they discover that the corn circles are not the only mystery at
the farm; a dilapidated barn conceals a terrifying secret. As
Midge and Ben uncover the true horror that is being spawned
there, they know that they must tell someone, warn them of
the danger. But who will believe their incredible story?

'Spine-chilling suspense' *Junior Education*

'Compelling' *The School Librarian*

**A FEDERATION OF CHILDREN'S BOOK
GROUPS PICK OF THE YEAR**

ISBN 0 440 86313 9

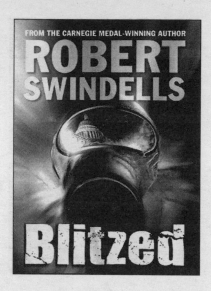

FROM THE CARNEGIE MEDAL-WINNING AUTHOR

ROBERT SWINDELLS

Blitzed

Imagine being alive before your parents were even born!

George is fascinated by World War Two – bombers, Nazis, doodlebugs.
Even evacuation and rationing has got to be more exciting than
living in dreary old Witchfield! He is looking forward to his school
trip to Eden Camp, a World War Two museum. But he doesn't
realize quite how authentic this visit to wartime Britain will be . . .

A hand reaching out of the fake rubble, a slip in time, and George
has to survive something much worse than boredom. The rubble
is now *real* – he has slipped through time into 1940s London!

A thrilling drama from a master of suspense, Robert Swindells.

'A first-rate time-travel story . . . Swindells is a powerful,
thrilling writer . . . as good as Robert Westall's classic,
The Machine Gunners.' *Independent on Sunday*

'Entertaining and thought-provoking . . . has a
wonderfully satisfying ending' *The Bookseller*

ISBN 0 440 86397 X

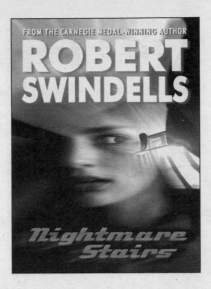

FROM THE CARNEGIE MEDAL-WINNING AUTHOR
ROBERT SWINDELLS

Nightmare Stairs

I'm falling . . . falling down steep, narrow stairs . . .
If I hit the bottom asleep, I know I'll never wake.

Every night Kirsty wakes up screaming. Every night she
has the same terrible nightmare – of falling downstairs.
But *does* she fall? Or is she *pushed*?

Then Kirsty discovers that her grandma died falling downstairs
and she begins to wonder. Is the dream hinting at a dark
secret in her family? She has to know the truth. But tracking
a murderer is a dangerous game, and as she delves into
the past, Kirsty uncovers a secret more terrible than
anything she can imagine . . .

'Cleverly put together . . . funny as well as gripping'
Sunday Times

**WINNER OF THE SHEFFIELD CHILDREN'S BOOK
AWARD FOR BEST SHORTER NOVEL**

ISBN 0 440 86330 9